PLAYS BY LAWRENCE KRAUSER

Honeymoon in Dealey Plaza
Wall Street Made Simple
A Virtual Deal
Horrible Child
Whale Tale

D1059007

McSWEENEY'S BOOKS
429 Seventh Avenue
Brooklyn, NY 11215

Published in the United States by McSweeney's Books

McSWEENEY'S and colophon are registered trademarks
of McSweeney's, a privately held company with
wildly fluctuating resources.

First published in the United States by McSweeney's, 2000

This is a work of fiction. Names, characters, places, and incidents are
either the product of the author's imagination or are used fictitiously.

Manufactured in Iceland by Oddi Printing

1   3   5   7   9   10   8   6   4   2

Library of Congress Cataloging-in-Publication Data
ISBN: 0-9703355-1-2

for Larissa

LEMON

I

Always comes from a different part of the ceiling, so it must be alive, whatever is making those rustling, scratching forays in the middle of the night. A mouse? A fervent, burrowing cockroach? Once in the Waning Days he woke to the stare of a red two-incher, remembers it as a scarab perched on the gleaming dune of her shoulder. Their eyes met, his two, its five, for a boggling second; then it was off skittering up her smooth sleeping neck, chin, cheek, disappearing into the forest of curls—into her ear? He'd fallen asleep wondering, then in the morning while she brushed her teeth caught a lobe between his lips and, feigning a kiss, peeped in hopeful for a glimpse of roach feet kicking. Would he have plucked the little beast out, or left it to steep in cerebral sauces? But he spied nothing.

Wendell's eyes are wide but look on darkness. When he wonders why the night after night of solitary boozing to the point of collapse, when he forgets the origin of the ritual, he lapses into sobriety and sleeps not deep enough to achieve oblivion of the overhead scratching.

= = =

On the day Marge split, on his rush up the stairs to stop her, he passed the exterminator, who told him she had already gone, in fact he'd helped her with her bags. Offered to spray but she'd said she had no time and anyway nothing she couldn't handle herself.

Wendell: Right. Me.

—Nah.

—Casual swat.

—I do your place?

—No thanks. Be wanting the company.

A weekday, it was, he'd been at the office counting commas on the screen, as usual stretching time until Candice starts to worry will her memo get written. Not enough work to justify his employment, so he tries not to be too fast. She likes having him there, but it puts her on the spot every time he finishes a task.

Breath warm on the back of his neck. Candice's chin docks at his shoulder. She peers at his PC screen: Is that for me?

—Of course.

She reads. Wendell rolls back in his chair, closes his eyes. After all, is it so surprising life exists? A symptom of motion, that's all; the problem is matter in general. Faint clanky punk-squeals from headphones in the next cubicle, Scott's. Candice absently humming along, as if it were her Easy Listening.

His eyelids part, reveal Michelle across the room, hunched heavy over her work. Asleep?

—Can I read it out loud? Candice is breathless.

—Uh—

—Michelle, Scott, you have to hear this memo Wendell wrote for me— How do I get to the top? [PAGE UP] Everyone listening?

Michelle blinking awake from her doze, Scott in a slow turn to face him, Candice explaining We all have something to learn from a Quality Memorandum, Michelle's eyes to Wendell's to steel herself against laughter, tries to pucker away a blooming grin.

> TO: PRESIDENT & CEO GREG FULLER
> FROM: CANDICE PREMISS
>
> Due to the recent election returns, in which as you know a certain someone was elected into a certain office, there will be some changes made in taxation policy, which are detailed in the chart below and hereby submitted for you *to review and amend as you see fit* [this phrase Candice likes, repeats] and return to myself via fax or interoffice mail . . .

Ceremonial but familiar feel, conversational yet to the point, even au courant.

—Wendell is that your phone?

Memo King still slave in speaking world. He picks up the call: Hello?

—I'm all packed and now I'm leaving.

—Marge?

—So long, Wendell.

—Wait—my letter?

> *Agree or disagree: If our relationship were the history of music, then we have not evolved beyond Mozart. We sit at the piano, twelve notes in octaves splayed before us— 88 keys, willing, potent! Our fingers move to play, and we deploy not even half the notes available. Our rhythm is boxy, our melody quaint, our harmony primitive*

—Ha!

—Marge?

—Do you stand by those words?

> *I can't speak for you. I suppose this is partly why I'm near despair. I had assumed that our union would mean I could take for granted our thinking would fuse; that we might live in a kind of inverse aboriginal state in which our minds, not in sleep but while awake, would be one*

—Don't you? I regret having to dis Mozart.

—Yeah, I imagine that'd hit you pretty hard.

> *I don't know what you hope for. Perhaps you see me as I do you, somewhere between a babbling brook and stagnant pond; there is stagnancy among us, Marge*

—Marge can I call you back in about five minutes—

Are you the same in your speech and in your thoughts?
Do you consider discrepancy there tenable?

He says goodbye to the dial tone, hangs up slow.

Candice sighs officially. It's so nice to see two young people—

—Can we finish this tomorrow?

—I thought it was.

—Needs a tweak.

—You two make me feel pretty gushy.

He grabs the phone again, dials. It rings and rings. He leaves the office. Ten minutes to get a cab. Her exit deftly timed to coincide with afternoon rush hour. On the radio of the taxi stuck in traffic, a militant cult member ranting: Oh yeah they'll tell you you've been brainwashed and you can say to them You bet I was and I'm glad, 'cause before it sure was dirty!

His letter to her a tight ball set deliberately on top of the answering machine, which has been turned off.

With these thoughts in mind, I've taken the liberty
of booking us a four-star hotel room for tomorrow
afternoon at two (see attached). An hour and arena
for the rivers of our private musics to merge. What do
you say? You show me yours, I'll show you mine?

Hell in ballpoint!

He burns it over the stove, watches the phrases curl black, modulate to smoke.

YOU'VE NEVER BEEN ABLE TO READ MY HANDWRITING, YOU'VE NEVER LEARNED TO READ IT, WHICH TO ME SAYS MORE THAN ANY NOTE COULD. Taped to the fridge like a holiday postcard. **I'LL TRY TO WRITE LEGIBLY FOR YOU, AS I WANT NO MISUNDERSTANDING,** at which point the handwriting turns complete Greek, and Wendell has Bill read him the rest during happy hour at Asylum, where the strangely narrow bartop has girth only for elbows; makes it difficult to bury head in arms. **TIRED OF AMADEUS? TRY LUDWIG: SO SOLL ES SEIN,** and she's sullied a great opus forever.

Must it be?

OK, Marge.

His eardrums feel like wet laundry but manage to thump out her dirge, then Bill talking a geyser of dung, solipsistic stabs at what's-to-be-wished-for. What does he know about it, he and Sally have been actualized mutually for a decade. **I FEEL SCRUTINIZED WHERE I**

WOULD PREFER DISINTEREST, AND IGNORED WHEN ATTENTION WOULD BE APT. I DO NOT SEEM ABLE EVEN TO BOIL A KETTLE OF WATER WITHOUT CRITICISM.

—Absolute gospel, he announces, but she changes the height of the flame as it heats up, starts with it low and increases it. What is that, I ask you?

Elbow sliding off the bartop, scraping painfully along its edge.

—PLEASE WATER MY PLANTS UNTIL I COME GET THEM.

—It's true we were semiotically incompatible.

—What the hell did you write her, man?

Tequila to the sky: To the progress of years! Drink up, aging organism. It Must Be.

When Sally arrives, she applauds the breakup: You thought you two had a quality rapport? Does anybody here think they had a quality rapport? And Nort behind the bar: People are like Rubik's Cubes, who you are depends on whose hands you're in.

—Yes like that bottle there please Cuervo if you would Nort thank you.

—Somewhere we're all pure, beautiful.

Come, tequila, come and I will twist you, I will shape your stuff to my purpose: a night of monogamy, you and I? Well he's through with all that, with all everything. Only oases now, pooling in his ears, and Marge's note running a bartop gauntlet of strangers' greedy eyes and greasy fingers.

Months later this will all have turned to blur, except for a single vivid moment: someone's hand, he can't tell whose, pushing toward him—*Here, chase that*—a saucer of lemon wedges, then Wendell's own hand rising into the frame of memory to set down with risky force the fresh-empty glass.

Leonardo da Vinci performed an autopsy out of sheer curiosity on a lifelong friend who had died just twenty minutes before, while they were chatting. Leonardo regarded any personal attachment as a displacement of his birthright share in the world, and frequently declared: A man alone, the whole world is his. Mated, he's only got half.

Out of the subway and onto a bus and over the river to Mom and Dad's and a dinner that's slow and somber and, he hears his parents thinking: Margeless. Salads are fiddled in silence as the minutes pass, funereal.

But stomachs know that life goes on. Salads are finished, pasta brought out and eaten with collective mute militance. He's deep into his meal when his father speaks the first words since they sat down: No wonder. Look how he eats.

—No wonder what?

—You don't use a fork?

—I'm not as charming as I used to be.

—Marge had great zest, says his mother.

His father's linguini, paused halfway to his mouth, unravels slowly back into its bowl. Empty fork into mouth. Metal on teeth. Marge was smart.

—That she was, says Wendell.

—She *was*, says his mother.

—Still is, I'd think.

—With her you were functional.

Divisional. Wendell in his pockets, digging. I'm sure she'd love to see y'all, I have the number where you can reach her, just a sec.

—A smart-aleck, this one.

—I got it here—

—All right, you had an argument. His mother leans toward him, quivering hope in soft tosses to his left eye, his right. You had problems? That can be worked on.

—Marge was a gem, says his father.

His mother sits back again, nodding. That's a very good word for Marge, gem. Doleful to her lap: the same word.

—Ma, the sauce is sensational.

—The sauce is the same.

—Scrumptious.

—All right tell us something else, says his father. Tell us what's going on in this young persons' world we should know about—

—Did you fight? Was there yelling?

—There's nothing to talk about. Wave pattern interference.

—Sit up.

Club soda with a slice of lemon is delicious, the most minimal of all flavored beverages.

—Was it discussed?

With a swat at the air, his father deduces him ditched: Can't you see it in his eyes? A unilateral decision.

—Wendell what's wrong—

—Ditched by a good woman.

Light and life at arm's length up against the burning chandelier. Twenty billion years ago, what was there in the Universe? Now: color, symmetry, form.

—Don't play with your food!

His mother's hand jerks suddenly to grab from his the lemon slice, but he yanks away and the fruit flicks straight up into the chandelier, dislodges a crystal droplet that falls slow as a leaf into the serving dish, hits with a hard splat, marinara spraying the table from the center like a Muyerbridge milkdrop but enormous, red, brutal. Crystal pieces tinkling. The family flecked with sauce. Mayhem of accusation, he's broken the lamp. No, it's all his mother yelling. His father sits still, reflective, says, These are dangerous times for a single man. You walk around, you're protected?

—[spoon-scooping crystal from pasta] Mom. I thought you said this was a vegetarian dish.

—There is fruit in my chandelier.

—He hasn't learned a thing.

Wendell stands on his chair to reaffix the crystal.

—In his shoes yet!

His father eckhems: Will you sit down when I speak to you! This is life and death I'm talking.

And in the crags of shimmering light, a wet bright wanderer twigged, shooting color through a jagged cloud. Pluck! Replace. Lick. You taste of high light places. Sit. Thing. What is a thing? That which I have a word for. That which is Out There. Inanimate entity. Crux.

—I don't think you read the paper.

—Dad, how old am I.

—He asks his father!

—Do try to remember it was partly through youth that I acquired my present age, son. I remember how remote the future can seem. But it gets here, Wendell. It Shall Arrive. Don't you go out and be foolish now.

—He wouldn't be foolish. He may be a fool—

—Case in point, Marge is gone! His intelligence is up for debate. I'm not talking sheepskin here [splayed hands smack the table] Latex! The silverware jumps.

Wendell rises and walks toward white-framed French doors and through them into the room containing his childhood piano. He pulls out the bench and sits. Limerick e-mail from Michelle in his head in his fingers in completely random notes in a ragtime rhythm:

> There once was a marine musician
> Who encountered a sailing statician.
> They met on a boat
> And agreed while afloat
> That the sea is a song to put fish in.

Behind him his father pulls double doors closed with sad mumblings. Wendell staining the keys with tomato sauce. The piano is a percussion instrument but with the skeleton of a harp. Wendell ends the rag in a sprinkle of lounge-lizard chords, fingers stiff from neglect, he fists and splays them several times, then lightly rests his fingertips on shellacked support wood. One finger rises and presses one key, keeps pressing, sustaining the sound. Not quite in tune, three strings wobble, braid in his ears. Any one note harbors within it all others, like white light enfolds the rainbow. Slow fade to the faint clinking of silverware, his parents clearing the table on the other side of the glass. The subtle fume of furniture polish.

His father's van, his father driving. Top Forty a bog of self-pollinating single cells. Wendell kills the dashboard radio. I am no realized prodigy, but still a man has ears. Earlier it rained, now we listen to the whoosh of cars on wet streets. Do you listen? There, nooked in a belly of grass, an anonymous building whose parking lot stirs memory.

—You think the piano needs tuning?

—That's just the way I play, Dad.

—No but when I play it I think it's out of tune. And those low notes are muddy.

—I think it sounds fine.

—I gotta get it tuned.

—Do you lie to people about what I do?

—Seatbelt.

A flashlight shining in on Wendell and Marge through the blue-tinted window of the van that is no longer shaking; the shaking is how they'd been found out. Wendell turns the ignition key to roll down the window, Marge pulling on her bra slowly cup by cup, eyeing the cop peering in, saying: What's the point of suburbs if you cannot fuck in your vehicle?

—*I'm sure I don't know, miss, but it's best not to park next to a hydrant. You Wendell?*

—*Uh.*

—*Recognize the van. Your father's a good man. How's the research going?*

—*What research?*

—*Things busy in the lab these days?*

—*I don't work in a lab.*

—*Listen, it runs in my family too, you can bet I'm rooting for you.*

—*All right.*

Thanksgiving, two years ago, or three, or more. His buttocks, home for the holiday, bare on vinyl, growing chilly from the cold night pouring in. A fine line between cozy demographics and love, history shows. Though not with groups. The windows of the van all steamed. Condensation to gather and drip into grass-green armrest fur, to burst forth come morning with the slam of the driver's door and mist his father in dank echoes of his son and only child's fruitless union. Kid's pushing middle age, humps with the modus operandi of a teenager. But

Dad's senses are trained to talk amongst themselves; a police report in the mail would likely prove more pungent than the afterwhisp of feral antics.

Marge to the cop: Mind shoving that light away from me? *{dexterous eyebrows arch and hood in the chaotic beam of the flashlight}*

Site of so much pleasure, now still as a ruin, though moving exactly at speed limit. Not a multipurpose let alone recreational vehicle.

—Never mind, says Wendell.

—Why did you ask me that?

—Really, it's OK.

—Tell me again what it is you do.

—Interdepartmental memoranda. Communications.

—This means?

—The world's problems. Triangles are good. There are special relationships.

—What are you talking about?

—I don't know.

—Screwball.

—We don't need to know in Payroll.

—The man's family actually involved?

—I think the president's his nephew, great nephew?

—Buckminster Full-of-it, snaps his father, goes on to speak of drug dens in Alaska built from parachute cloth stretched over vast lattice of welded crowbars, plans to cover entire cities in such webbing so they can detach from the planet and float self-sustaining through space, a man who from birth preserved every letter, laundry receipt, parking ticket, every single document he ever encountered that had his name on it—and now, decades after his death, tax dollars still support the logging of his mania. A man who persisted in his folly, for what.

—You ever hear him speak, Dad?

—Never.

—They play videotapes of his lectures in the lobby, this giant video screen.

—What does he say?

—He talks very quickly, lots of gesturing. I'm always fishing for my ID.

—They're subliminally indoctrinating you.

—Lot of people stop and listen, visitors, tourists come in.

—You should know the people you're working for.

I should know more about this world, about my life. But you see a building go up, its plodding progress toward heaven month after month through laps of seasons until complete—one more deliberate act on the accidental earth. If it had one day simply appeared, regal and inexplicable. Or if it had always been there?

—So Dad. I heard this interesting thing, these two guys on line at a donut stand. They were talking about the war. Vets, these guys.

—Which war?

—I'm not sure, it's not crucial, they were discussing this incident—

—Not crucial, he says.

—They had two rows of American soldiers lined up, the enemy did I mean—

—All wars the same in your mind, Wendell?

—Prisoners of war, all of them on their knees with their hands tied behind them, they're in these parallel rows on their knees facing out. Dad?

Stopped near the bridge where his father customarily drops him to catch a bus into the city. But I am talking, Dad. I know: you wonder if my anecdote will have a shape. You are skeptical.

—Hell, I'll drive you in.

The car moves into traffic, through a tollbooth, both of them silent until halfway over the moon-ribboned river, the city a brilliant tiara before them.

—This is a joke you're telling.

—No, it was these guys. So the two enemy soldiers are strolling up and down between these rows of American POWs, and every few minutes one of the enemy fires his gun into the back of the head of one of the Americans. Totally arbitrary, guy falls out of the line dead. They can't kill all of them, because they need some to bargain with, but they can spare a few for the sport. All of a sudden one of these prisoners jumps up and bolts, his hands tied behind him, he's running and yelling at the top of his lungs. Nobody gets it, they just can't believe it, the enemy guys look at each other like what the hell, then one nods to the other, very polite, the second guy lifts his rifle and blows the American away. While he's running. In one shot.

—Of course.

—Of course, but—the guy who was running had to have known he was going to be shot. They had to shoot him. He must have *wanted* to be shot.

—So?

—Right?

—This story has meaning for you?

—What?

—Suicide, Wendell. That's called suicide.

—I don't know.

Outside it drizzles. His father hits the wipers, tries several speeds, settles on slow mist.

—You get it, Dad? He wasn't running for his life—

—Wendell, you are facing bachelor days, you'll have time on your hands, I suggest you read in history.

The miles go by.

—*Orgasms too on point-scales?*

—*Of course!*

—*Strip them of their precious selfhoods, fling them into ghettoes of criteria?*

—*Please, suh.*

—And about Marge.

—Thanks, Dad.

His father drops him off on his corner and drives away. Wendell walks the half-block to his building and opens the outside door and nearly trips over a lemon on the floor of the tiny foyer. He picks it up and pockets it. Lest the less-nimble injure themselves.

A low thrum in his gut. Love. What is the measure of such a thing? Love, or the word love, is like an elusive jungle bird that because it is so durable has thousands of mimics and camouflaged neighbors.

The tree of the lemon is self-fruitful, needing no other. Grown from seed, it begins to bear in its seventh year. Seeds remain viable for up to six months after removal from the fruit. The tree blooms best when planted on a slope to receive the fullest sun, shielded from wind, up out of the cold air that settles in valleys. In the hottest climes pruning must be judicious, as the bark is easily sunburned. The lemon tree absorbs radiated heat from the soil during cool nights. Smudge pots may be beneficially set underneath its branches; the resultant convection will prevent the coldest air from settling on the leaves. Though more tolerant of cold than all other citrus, one hour in sub-freezing temperature can injure small ones. But a moderate amount of moderate cool before they ripen does wonders for their lemonness, increasing the acid level—a commercial plus. Excessive heat and/or humidity tends to bring out the sweetness, confusing consumers. The West has generally tartened all strains, dried and darkened them, and curbed by a quarter their trees' potential for twenty-foot heights. The lemon tree sprouts reddish leaves that lighten to sea green and birth white flowers. A respectable annual yield is fifteen hundred lemons per plant, but this rate may double in perennially mild climes. Lemons are best picked while still green and bursting with aminoes, allowing for future ripening in transport.

And when I come into your presence, do you brighten? Does your attention vex or cave? Is the air between us animate? We were segments along a circle thinking ourselves straight, acting accordingly. Now, from a distance: anything learned? "Progress." Bah! The past is fractal premonition, infinite to the eye but nothing to be built on, an itchy scalp that in scratching scatters a dandruff of words never to be appeased, ever inflating in need, words like currency to be spent in definition, squandered in reflexive use; know the market and keep mum. Meaning is fickle and subject to will. Love? Sin? Self? Numbness abounds, the curse of the courtiers; patience and imagination are cross-the-board sapped. What could cure us will never catch on, probably be mistaken for the original evil itself. Too bad: would force away triscuit grapplements, restore the shock of being. Penicillin for the children!

Zap screen. Memo macro. Snapshot of Marge's arms around a snowman outside a log cabin atop some mountain. I don't ski, why should I weekend with skiers? Twisted his ankle chicly the first morning not seeing where the edge of the porch was. Marge didn't ski either, why was she there, then? They met. Remained in the cabin alone an extra three days in a duet orgy of acquaintance. Hot chocolate and rum, a floor heater and their minds a wide field, something fugal blasting on the stereo, always beginning. Snow falling past all the windows.

—*And while it cannot be said that I am the most qualified of those who aspire to this great office*

—*Nor the most visionary*

—*Or reactionary*

—*Or preservatory*

—*Nor the most intelligent, perhaps*

—*Indeed not measurably the most educated*

—*While it cannot be denied that I am in the final analysis the least appropriate candidate among us*

—*No doubt whatsoever I am a total fool*

—*No doubt I am in no way fit to govern*

—*It is however more than clear that I am, with no remotely near second, the indisputably most physically beautiful candidate in the running*

—*Just to look at me is to set the optical nerves tingling with delight*

—*Just watch me gesticulate, symmetrically, with both hands*

—*That's no coincidence!*

Wendell, says Michelle.

—Yeah.

—Scrap the photo.

—I think the Universe wants us to kiss.

So when then did tongues turn to swords touching at their points, blades buckled in the instant of thrust to scrape loose and plunge forward, dangerous? Eye contact was at last like that, a finite lunge and hold, no parry; the next move would snub the gaze. What is the monster from legend that cannot die till looked directly in the eye, or was it from a nightmare of his own? One of them would subtly shift, try to spot other than the offered facet—the connection would snap. Just to blink prompted defense. Action and reaction rippling out uncontrollably. Only rigidity could bring us to calm.

—And how are we doing here? [nailpolish cool through aged flannel on shoulder] How are you feeling? asks Candice.

Stay alert. Frequent Freakout miles to be eked. Let voice waver.

—I'm a little . . . No, it's nothing.

—Are you having a Marge Day?

—Maybe I am.

—Sometime we'll have to take lunch, I'll tell you about my own love life, make you feel like a lucky man.

The soul of the acorn pulls it into an oak, the ideal congeals the Revolution. And you, you always hedged. What was it—good days, bad, hours of rising stakes and rushing wins and falls, a creeping despair, realizing: there is no unseen benevolent hand. Then why does my heart beat one more time? Why is the speed of light what it is? Why is it always the same? Gallop, lope, disunited canter, a rabbly road of words. What did we ever talk about. From lubricating time to pointillist daubs to the ceaseless groan of rusting gears, the entire militia of our status quo, mobilized. Was this how it was? Can't remember any of it.

Continuously playing in the lobby this month is a series of lectures, some as much as twelve hours straight, delivered by Buckminster Fuller:

> Experience suggests to me that we really won't find a hole through those stars till I finally get through a billion times one hundred billion stars that surround us, that we now know of already. If I were to take the number of atoms in this room surrounding us here, and in these pretty thick walls, I'd get into that kind of number. So that I probably wouldn't find any hole out in the stars . . .

—Take a look at my leading opponent
—A foul-looking critter if ever there was
—Woulda thought someone would have have taken him aside
and said something
—Kid, you're just not cut out for politics
—I know I'm overweight. But that doesn't make me smart.
Ask yourselves: Haven't we had enough wit and ability?
—It's time for a true nitwit
It was a game! Wasn't it?

Wendell sleeps, steeped in his past, a gray room, cold, lined with freezers. The experimental frozen-soup detail crowding an oblong table passing small white cartons to the left, each person adding a precise amount of peas/corn/pasta then passing to the left, to the left, Wendell to measure out twelve shells of pasta one thousand times a day, which he does until the day he spots tiny spiders dead in tiny pasta coffins. He alerts the supervisor. Each employee at the table a temp and so loses two shifts' pay while the company investigates. Silent treatment for Wendell upon return to gig.

Wendell no longer eats shell pasta, but bugs continue to tomb his life. Open group burials in the sinks and fridge egg holders that are not fairly blamed on Wilhelm, his new roommate, all port and priss and eye-itching fluff. I am no natural cat-sitter. Will Bill and Sally ever return? Why leave Aruba?

No, not fair to blame the beast. Everything for months this way, brutal mayhem everywhere lurking. Don't whizz fuzzball scapegoat too hard across the room. Skewed its meows to maraca-toothed wimpers last night upon waking to his biceps being suckled in frantic shameless need. Why must they be forever waking him up in the middle of the night? These living things?

Away! Eleven years old and still nursing incorrect objects. Mount your phantom females, boy. *An even mix of dry and wet. Change the litter alternate days.* Fond memories. Takeout remains for him now, or the growing unidentified strata in the kitchenspace sink. Catfood uneaten crusts quickly. The beast has taken to shitting in Marge's flowerpots, which now serve also for ashtrays. Smoking, a new habit, helps to camouflage moister odors, and ensures that the pilot light is exercised, as he does not own a pack of matches. Make a note: acquire matches. **WATER THE PLANTS.** What's that you say? Simple enough; ah well. If you come intent on rescue, you will see the crops have been rotated. Fertilized with premium cat dung, my cigarette ends have rooted and are sprouting extra-tall deep-flavored nonfiltereds with whiskers and a longstem pipe. Nicotine the oldest insecticide—this place will be a paradise! Wendell had hoped to sic Wilhelm on the scratcher in the ceiling, but the pussy is as ineffective as he is. Together they lie in bed, necks craned up like tennis fans' at a lob that never falls.

Awakens in the morning to feline famished yowls. Animal on his chest poking his cheek with a nose that is wet and cold. Hurls the cat across the room, sits up. Something odd around the left eye and mouth. Heaviness. Yawning—tight. He looks in the mirror to see that the port side of his face is completely inert. Will not respond to orders. Meow. He pulls at his cheek, presses his lips together, tries to smile, to close his left eye but it just springs open again. Thwacks his cheek: the skin is sensitive. Meeoooow. But the muscles seem dead. Meeeeeeeooo— *What, what?* Fruit Loops to shut the nag up. Moistens them with tap water, then back in bed shutting wayward eye with a finger, sets the clock radio for an hour away, falls asleep easily. Wakes to Muzak Hendrix, nearly crushes the radio but his fist lands on a corkscrew. Littered labyrinth to bathroom mirror.

Same thing. Half his face a carnival mask of astonishment. No pain, no movement.

He should. He phones the office.

—Payroll.

—Candice, this is Wendell.

—Wendell! You sound strange.

—I can't move the left side of my face.

—My God! Did you call someone?

—I look kind of scary, I think.

—Call a doctor right now! It sounds like a stroke!

—You think?

—Do you want me to come over?

—No that's OK, I feel OK.

But if it's a stroke, time will be of utmost essence and I can have a day off with pay.

In five minutes he is dressed and in a crosstown cab moving through a glorious sunshower. He rolls down the window, tilts his face to catch the rain. Then lingers outside the emergency room loving the warm wet light, considers not going in. A ghoulish reflection flashes in a revolving door: him. He goes in.

His doctor is a slim man with big spring-curled hair, twice
Wendell's age but shames him with vigor and the remark:
You could stand to lose some weight.

—What about you? How do you stay so thin?

—Me? I have no time to eat.

Wendell being kneaded. Thighs, testicles, kidneys,
thyroid, cheeks. This man's health tangible and exasperated
in his fingertips.

—You smoke?

—Well—

—Yes.

—Just a couple of weeks.

—You are a smoker.

Wendell explains how he is on the verge of stopping
because everything hurts, his chest, his throat, but they don't
hurt quite bad enough, but they almost do. Half remembers
a Chinese maxim: Worst something best something out of
difficult something.

—Uh-huh. Why did you start?

—You think it's related to my face?

—Two symptoms with a common cause, maybe. Drink? Sure you do. What's your poison?

—Depends.

—Won't be helpful.

—Well not every day.

—Good.

Every night. Wendell asks if he's had a stroke. The doctor tells him he will if he keeps smoking. Your sonogram shows you have a mitral-valve prolapse.

—What's that?

—An aberrance in the structure of your heart. Nothing half my ballet dancers and basketball players don't have, so you're in good company. One of your heart's valves is longer than is usual. Not a big deal; genetic. Ever do cocaine?

—Once.

—You're lucky to be alive. For you it's Russian Roulette.

—But my face—

—Not related. Pinched nerve. Stress. Take it easy, you'll be back to normal in three months.

—Three months!

—You complaining?

—No.

—Spare me. There are plenty of people out there in some very bad situations, and you are not one of them.

Wendell is presented with a black eye-patch. Until you can blink again. Doctor's orders: Relax. Wendell puts the patch on and walks around the room as instructed for ten minutes to adjust. He pauses in front of the mirror, tries to see that it is him. No way.

On the way out he takes a couple of paper-wrapped candies from the bowl on the receptionist's desk. He is smiled at. Wendell is not facially capable of returning a full smile, even if he should wish to. When the elevator doesn't come immediately, Wendell, restless, steps into the stairwell and from there through a window onto the fire escape, where he lights a cigarette and looks with one eye at what the building tops reveal of the sky.

There was a time when our desire for each other would have landed us in an asylum or prison, had it not been sanctioned by mutual assent. True or false.

In a flash sees himself: an unwashed slouched stranger in an eye-patch, smoking on a fire escape while casing the rears of buildings for possible break-in opportunities. Snubs out the cigarette on the brick wall behind him, climbs back in through the window and takes the stairs down.

On the street, he unwraps a candy and places it on his tongue. His mouth floods with luke letdown. Why this insistence on names that bear no relation to the attributes of the product? An appliance is one thing, but a flavor is a promise that melts right in your mouth. Not a wisp of citrus tang. Saccharin, synthetic, unsuckable. Got a lemon at home. Wish I had it on me now. Bite right through the rind.

= = =

On a wall panel in the subway car: ONE OUT OF EVERY TEN AMERICANS SUFFERS FROM MENTAL DISEASE, call this number and tell all your friends. The man on his left: Ain't it the truth. The woman on his right: Yeah? What's wrong with you? The man on his left: I can't remember birthdays.

The man with the deformed heart and lopsided face approaches his illegally sublet brownstone. His heart beats despite itself, pushes blood to deaf nerves flying loose in wet windy alleys. His mouth, oblivious, adrift, sags. His legs scissor, his brain ticks. No trace of rue or cheer about his faulty body. His body changes, his mind comments, or does not comment; why bother with opinion or mood? What I think changes nothing. An intention fulfilled is an intimation confirmed. The weather's gone cold, the leaves all off the trees, blowing brown and dry through east-west streets. Life is the head of foam on a Big Beer poured long, long ago, a frothy chaos.

—*NEVER!*

Gloria as usual leaning on her cane on the corner under the deli's blue awning, scowling up storms. *Never talk to you again! Never talk to ME again!* He tries to pass without being seen. But it's him she's talking to. No, she's talking to a car, I am invisible. Pain and pleasure are all one to this walking, thinking man. The world will fit itself to any thought; the art is in the commentary. Things continue, named, unnamed. *Get away from me!* I am seen.

Jowls shaking, her eyes laser the ground between them.

—Gloria, how are you.

—*TERRIBLE, I can hardly walk, try to sue, don't nobody listen! I got leaflets to prove it. Tried to pray—nothin'! I say Jesus I need you NOW, I look around—nothin'! and I love that man, he my NIGGER, talk to that sumbitch every day'a my life. Do he talk back, NO he don't, MAYBE he do but he pick the wrong TIME.*

Wendell in fitter moods relishes her speech, its sliding and swooping from nostalgia to fury to suspicion like great jazz. But tonight he inches forward toward home as she rants. *Gotta spaz be a plumber, gotta mailman for a blind man, fifty bats in an air conditioner, that thing so broke, so broke, so—* Her jaw falls, she stares straight at him: *Devil heaven wrong wit' YOU?*

She peers at his face. The novelty of her open interest in an organism other than her own gives him a fleeting—joy, is it? The knotted pucker that is her general expression relaxes and in an instant she looks a half century younger and vulnerable.

It is dusk. Wendell angles his head to better catch the storelight, peels up his new black eye-patch.

Gloria laughs short and loud, stomps the sidewalk with her cane. *You the ugliest cat on the BLOCK! On Saturday it was I think was Saturday it was I walked down to that street down there, didn't see nothin' like what I see right now, what you call in the profession Somebody Was Not LOOKING. They broke that mold right over yo' head! Up and down, make no difference, can't even look at what I'm lookin' ugly UGLY! What happened, you find religion?*

—My baby done left me.

—Skinny Lady?

Don't stop walking, is the trick; he pivots and continues slowly backward, says: Yeah.

She cackles and jigs. *Speak to my hand, child, speak to my HAND! Give a woman time and she always leave a man, I seen it before, I done it before, gimme the chance and I'll do it right now, joy'a wisdom and the breath'a God, don't even need my cane, YAHOO! A person has a leg and a leg hurt, sad and sorry, fit and tender don't make no difference, GIMME that thing.*

Her cane spins to a stop on the sidewalk. Wendell retrieves it, hands it to her.

—Have a good night, Gloria, rest well.

—Rest don't excite me, I'll tell you what excite me, NOTHIN' excite me. My sister died.

—Gloria—I'm so sorry. How?

—Dropped dead at the fuckin' supermarket.

—Oh, no. When?

—Six years ago Thursday. You know what they said at her funeral? Never Said Nothin' Bad About No One. Ain't that the truth. That what killed her.

Before Marge: youth's days of hopeful abandon. For erotic ambience, the simple joy of simply living, his preferred haunts were: small chic bookstores. Many an hour swelled and sighed in fine shops striking poses with hefty latest in hand. Rosy light kissing polished woods, air agurgle with cellos and violas and murmurings helpful and grateful.

Did he read there? But who could scrunch an iris in such lushness? Well: those he came to be near. Mere proximity satisfied. More to do, he suspected, with the carnality of a focused gaze, like that of the bellydancer, than with subtle/savvy front-lobe antics. Of course it has turned out that the hot highbeam of bibliomania does not necessarily transpose into life in general, because for instance Marge was a big reader, she was always having insights, constantly, and every time she did her eyes would shift, as if each new thought were an object suddenly appearing in the room. And yes, the various categories of thinking affect eye-movement, and moods can be induced merely by changing the angle of a glance, yes this is unexplored and promising therapeutic terrain, nevertheless it is irritating to be in the constant company of someone so obviously cognating at every opportunity, not from necessity but from habit, I swear, since after all what else can it be that keeps a mind in motion, predictable as the skeleton of a snake?

But back then— What's this? A gorgeous small book new-arrived on the shelves, the cumulative plane of the ends of its pages ripply with knowing texture. An author photo of such profound sensuality, he half expects psalms inside. Lives in this city. He writes to her, gushes pages of baseless praise—

> *So what does it feel like, to hold the Great Torch?*
> *Clearly your palms do not easily scorch!*

—sends it care of her publisher. It is only when she replies by postcard to his letter—

> *A coffee for two*
> *e.g., me and you*
> *would please at least one*
> *who is glad you had fun*
> *perusing her poems*
> *i.e., the hat-hung homes*
> *of her wandering pen...*
> *Coffee? Dim-sum?*
> *Where? When?*

—that he returns to the bookstore and opens her book and finds he can't understand a thing. Paragraphs set in shapes of animals and mathematical figures. Pages with only one word, or one word in each corner. And when they meet at a Chinese restaurant, her speech resembles her poems—disconnected phrases that flare briefly in sharp but oblique directions—which makes him feel safely invisible in a foreign land. Wendell is the world, the world is him, he is adrift and wind-drunk and open to life. They go to her apartment where she shows him watercolors she has painted to accompany her poems. Her publisher hadn't thought them professional enough for her book, but to Wendell's relief here are simple and identifiable forms, credible animals and human faces. He relaxes, able to praise with sincerity. She is pleased.

—*Shall we consult the thesaurus of the body?*

Weeks of evenings without complexity or evolution. Then she left town on a travel grant and he took over her apartment. A few months turned to a year, now almost eight years. Between them things cooled rapidly once she began to travel, then over the years gradually, then altogether. Where she is now, he has no idea. She used to write him once in a while to ask him to send her furniture, paintings, books; and thus the apartment grew steadily less hers, more his, then when Marge was there very much hers, now less hers, too.

Enough global awareness to not throw away aluminum, plastic, glass, but not enough local will to rinse or collect, so they gather and gather. Mustn't forget his possessions are nine tenths of the law. His deep-down feeling of no rightful claim to the place keeps him from calling the super for repairs. Entropy's hit quite a stride lately with no one or nothing to oppose it. The living room ceiling paunches curiously on one side, sagging closer each year, adding to the concentric hypertrophy. Three of the square-foot plasterboard tiles have fallen to the floor, fortunately or unfortunately on no one's head, and the resultant gape reveals what he suspects might be a board of asbestos. The kitchenspace faucet drips a constant pulse, if he had a piano he could practice scales to it, for some reason slightly faster in hot weather. Otherwise the sink is dormant. The toilet running loudly without a break, once in a while filling over capacity so that Wendell wakes up or returns from work to find an inch of cold water on the bathroom tiles, his downstairs neighbor in damp spirits banging with a broom on the floor between them. In the period when he and Marge would still occasionally phone to stem a disaster, the superintendent—possibly aware of their fraudulent tenant status—seemed to go out of his way to offend whenever possible. In the place to do some work, he'd use the bathroom and not flush, leave stinking cigarette butts in the bathtub and sometimes a grimy rag or bar of wet soap right on a couch cushion. Marge believed that he once was very rude to her verbally, but couldn't be certain because of his thick and unusual accent. Wendell asked him where he was from, thinking to break some ice, sometimes all people want is to be known, but he only scowled and flashed an ID. Marge maintained that there are places on earth where such behavior would indicate warmth and familiarity, which goes a long way to explain strife among nations.

The gods of sleep hark not.

An inventory of the bod. Something wrong at every chakra, a sweeping capitulation. Couple months of cigarettes ineptly smoked? Think emptiness, you are all but solid. Must pee. Hysterical banging and braying waterpipes in this cranky old building. Is this where errant physiology begins, in shudders invading sleep? Bad data entering at tenderest moments? Wendell slides back into a leg of bumpy slumber, is woken by an adamant bladder.

Petulant meows in the darkness, furry thumps behind him as he stumbles into the bathroom and nearly trips over a plunger stuck in the middle of the floor. Nine days is not enough time, he knows from experience, in which to suffocate a roach. So the one caught now under the rubber cup, the one he trapped yesterday morning, faces a ten-day confinement. Flips on the fluorescent, made violent by medicine-chest mirrors. Careful around the plunger. Mustn't upset the experiment. Sits on the toilet and leans forward to grout the rim of rubber with toothpaste. Should ensure no extra oxygen gets in via cracks in the tiles.

On the way back to bed Wendell catches sight of the moon in his path, warm in color as if just risen. Nearly three quarters full, looking almost reachable there in the spilled light from the bathroom door. And indeed, Wendell can pluck it from the sky, and he takes it back to bed and falls asleep with his cheek pressed against its cool, cratered surface.

In the morning he doesn't see it immediately. Turns his head on the pillow to check the time, and there it is. Sitting up, he chucks it across the room (while it is airborne his clock radio clicks on; no matter how clear the signal when set, it's always white noise in the morning) into a pile of dirty but not unusable laundry. The lemon's thumpy landing startles a dozing Wilhelm, who trots over to the clothes, nosing for the source of the noise; but it's sunk.

TO: All Employees
FROM: The Ministry of Causality
RE: The Sinistry of Casuality

Every thought has its thump. Mind to the body is like a teabag to water. Secondhand indiscretion can be dangerous. One person's idle chatter is the next person's undoing.

In the beginning was the Word and the Word was God, but the Word was smashed to bits at Babel and history since has been the plucking-out of spoken shrapnel, shards of shattered symbols—a diurnal self-surgery for which there is no anesthesia.

And thus I propose that speech be restricted to a pragmatic minimum of relevant facts and only the most essential endearments.

On Wendell's first day at this job there was a fellow in Payroll who took him aside and said, *Just for the record. This is not summer camp. I have a perfectly satisfying social life on the outside. I work here to make money, not friends. That said, it's nice to meet you.* At the time Wendell thought him cold, but over the years he has come to feel pretty much the same way. Yet he is also aware of a gossipy/confessional aspect to his own nature, which he takes pains to monitor closely, lest he overstep the boundary he would like others to observe. Whenever he does cross this line—inevitable in such close and frequent quarters—afterward he feels vaguely nauseous. And if when passing someone in the hall they say *So long, I'm off to root canal*, he returns to his desk and opens the Payroll Department Manual to its babbling lists of routing instructions and ID codes, to wash away images of the almost-stranger unconscious under bright lights, drool on chin.

Something stirs behind him. Undo, Undo, Swivel. Although baboons smile to express hostility, baring the incisors, this is only Michelle, sapient, saying: Peace and Love. Wendell wonders, not for the first time, Am I emitting a hippie vibe? Remembers a few days previous, an anonymous two-finger Peace sign wagging from inside an elevator as the doors closed.

No good. Hair may be getting out of hand. Not much in the groom's mood lately. A quick stroll past Accounting where a hall mirror does not reassure. That silly hemifrozen puss and his hair straggly, stringy. Marge used to corner and assault him with shears to stem the growth, which now is spiraling out behind him in the air-vent breezes. Coffee on yer collar, matie. Classic rogue accouterment, the patch. Have you ever kissed a man with no depth perception? Almost conceals his entire limp hemisphere. Behind it the eye is sweaty and itchy and moist, and he has to reach in several times an hour to press down the lid, which when left alone tends to spring open like that of a ventriloquist's dummy.

Back to the office. Stick-Em yellow not as yellow as the yellow arc of lemon flying across the room. Wendell takes care to explicitly remind his coworkers that stress is harmful to his health. Everyone is very gentle. He e-mails Michelle:

You can bet where there's wet there is water
And a woman of woman's a daughter
But how to be sure
What a sureness is for
When a surety than sooth is shorter?

Her reply:

10 to 1, land that's rich in conviction
Crops a bumper of people in friction
That's what sure's for
It guarantees war
The more sure's the sorer affliction.

—Is Marge there?

—No, she doesn't live here anymore.

—Is there a place I can . . . ?

—She's at her sister's, I think.

—Do you have that number?

—No, I lost it, sorry. Who's calling? If I speak to her I can give her a message.

—We wanted to see if she was still interested in doing some volunteer work for our agency.

—Wait, I'll find a pen.

It takes him a minute, then the pen doesn't work, so he pretends to take the information down. I'm sorry, could you spell that out?

Acronyms followed Marge like gnats, welcome gnats, pet gnats always flying in her ears, out her mouth, she loved their social lubricacy, resented his impatience with them, once held her speech hostage for the better part of an evening, refusing to utter another word until he unpacked some nonce she'd tossed off that he hadn't recognized, and which she couldn't get over him not knowing. They were at a restaurant. It was embarrassing, the stupid standoff in public. Wouldn't even open her mouth when the waiter came over, instead pointed in silence at her menu choices, then later at empty glasses to request refills. It was funny at first, then began to seem bizarre—she was genuinely upset. When he finally cracked the code, he retaliated by not proving it, insisting she trust him when he said he now knew what she was talking about. *An international conglomerate of nations toward a noble end* was all he'd fess. Still she would say nothing. Finally he spelled it out on the tablecloth with index finger and tartar sauce, which caused her to stand up and walk out of the restaurant, for which he had adored her.

He hangs up. The phone had woken him from what he'd hoped would be a true night's sleep. Oh well. Two days until paycheck. What's an insomniac to do?

Tucked among the clutter on the floor between couch-end and wall is a primitive television. Abandoned property of the poet; she'd pointed at it, said: Know your enemy. A potential companion. Did Marge even know we had this? She'd lobbied hard for a set. He digs toward it. His traces are not terribly moist or pungent; still the waft is clear. Spilt coffee, bourbon, soy sauce. Lotus-like bunches of dustballs afloat on a stagnant chaos, his pond of plastic spoons. And a VCR, wow. Modern me! He flails for an outlet close enough so that he won't have to move the set, a cartonlike thing he can reach from the couch by lying on his stomach with his chin propped on the arm—ouch, worn to the wood—he fetches a pillow. Finds the outlet, clicks on. Ceiling scratcher fast at it, Wilhelm at another altitude also scratching. Cat, hither! Crouch and be renamed: Frump. Where's that lemon. He digs and snags it from the laundry heap and flops onto the couch with the fruit held to his nostrils. Slow tubes and faint siren of ancient TV. Lemon on the pillow leaning against his nose.

Horrible reception on the dust-caked set. A narratoid static, something about the Arctic's bald eagles, blue bears, whales, all of which look crazily endangered through the snow of the whacked TV.

But the Aurora Borealis is beautiful through white noise, more breathtaking than he's ever seen it on any working set, or even at the movies.

Day Ten: Wendell yanks the plunger up from the floor and the insect charges out as if the time in solitary with no oxygen has only refreshed it. Maybe need a different grout, maybe fluoride is like orgone to bugs.

So. If there is nothing evident in a given solid mass to predict its attraction to and for another solid mass (this according to Buckminster Fuller, who couldn't be more emphatic and clear as he drives the point home to the studio audience); if this attraction is knowable only through observation of both masses in proximity to one another; if even then the attraction remains mysterious to science; if life is at its fundamental level a finite set of discrete bodies identical to those composing the corresponding level of all nonlife; if life and nonlife are indistinguishable at that level—

—Watch where you're walking, guy.

—Thank you.

There are people in the hallway who as they pass cause his limbs, in small but unmistakable degrees, to move. His swinging arm subtly levitates, contrary to gravity and to the tug of his stride, toward these people as they approach; or he teeters subtly away, elbow or shoulder brushing the wall. And they, the others, react similarly. Trajectories bend, shoes stutter on carpet.

He turns a corner on the way to the Xerox room, walks halfway down the hall while reading over the page to be reproduced. Glancing up, still walking, he recognizes a woman from Personnel whose name he doesn't know but who for months has with her gait and smiles consistently moved to motion his limbs in the halls, sometimes provoking exquisite minor arousals. At the moment she is leaning over an open file drawer in the office at the far end of the hall, back toward him. As he approaches she bends further over, and the hem of her already short skirt—much too short for the weather, never mind the job, and gauzy—lifts to reveal more and more of the backs of her thighs; and then, to his astonishment, there gradually appear the bottom crescents of her buttocks and the peep of panties drawn up between them. He expects her to catch herself immediately and straighten up, but instead she continues to bend, and soon Wendell finds himself beholding full half of a very bare bottom. Taut life beaming under fluorescents. If thine eye— I did not give myself eyes. Eye. And then she abruptly shuts the drawer, stands straight, turns around and sees him.

She smiles warm, unself-conscious. Nice patch, she says. Wendell nods, continues on his way. At the Xerox machine he pauses to consider. He has enjoyed the experience, which was unusual, dramatic to be sure; and its undeniable theoretical eroticism has got his mind buzzing. But where is the proportionate physiological response? His heart is calm, his groin quiet. Wendell muses that if this had happened a few weeks ago, it might have taken half an hour to regain his present level of composure. Also worth pondering, ordinarily, would be whether she had been at all conscious of him watching her, whether the rare display had contained an aspect of awareness on her part. Absorbed as he was in his memo for the first leg of the trip down the hall, he had no way of knowing whether she'd seen him coming. But he finds he doesn't much care. He has a complex task to do, two one-sideds to one two-sided, one of them Auto Contrast to clean a smudged fax, plus a 22-percent size reduction, times three hundred. He aces it in one smooth shot.

Flyers posted in the company cafeteria announce the anniversary of the third naturally formed carbon structure known to man (after graphite and diamonds) being christened buckminster-fullerine, or "Bucky Balls," after its form—a sphere whose surface is meaningfully faceted like a soccerball. Named "Molecule of the Year" by *Eye-On* magazine, Bucky Balls went on to claim the Nobel Prize, and Marshall McLuhan dubbed Buckminster Fuller "the Leonardo of our times." According to the flyer, which features extensive quotes from the magazine's interview with Buckminster's great-nephew, CEO Greg Fuller of Fuller Communication Company, Inc., the molecule's discovery

"validates my great-uncle's lifelong mission, I would even call it a crusade, to assert the primacy of certain structures in nature . . . [He] was, as you know, inventor of the ecologically tactful, geometrically beautiful, aesthetically minimal geodesic dome, whose importance to humanity was recognized first by our military, which is so often chief in prescience when it comes to secular advancement. Not that Bucky endorsed war, of course, he thought it was downright silly. But he could sure build a [heck] of a tent. They used a couple on Everest. Bucky also invented a three-wheeled car, in which he once gave Amelia Earhart a lift not very far from Boston."

Dry half peel on black street pavement just off the corner sidewalk curb, soot gray and jaundice motley, I'll throw you out proper, I do.

Sally and Bill are back from Aruba aglow with the half-life of leisure. A zealous health blasts Wendell from across the small round café table, giving him a headache that conspires with his eye-patch-nulled spatial intelligence to tip his cup repeatedly, at identical wrong instants, and dribble espresso down his shirt. He moves his tie again but can no longer conceal all the stains. Musters ostensible marvel for his friends' tale of a silky-coat toy poodle sold on the black market by Venezuelan Indians to a certain genre of tourist, he does not grasp the details of the sexual delicacy in question.

The conversation moves closer to home, then comes a moment of confusion in which Wendell agrees to go on a blind date with someone his friends think would be just perfect.

Slipped carpe diem into me cup, eh? But it has worn off by the time he gets home. Looks in the mirror. A date with my face in this condition? The stress could be disastrous. At least Bill and Sally will be there too. One week until guillotine.

But days seem strangely longer lately, in spite of the fast-coming winter; more than the sum of their hours. And there have been swollen moments. A few days ago, while clipping fingernails in the early evening, he found himself repeatedly distracted by the lemon, which had found its way to the kitchenspace counter and nestled amid ancient spastics of silverware. Will eyes always gravitate to the most sunlike thing? Finally he stopped trying to resist, let himself just watch it, seemed to sense something aligning around it. Then the phone rang. A shocking interruption. In fact, so acute was his concentration on the lemon, and so left-field harsh the ringing of the phone, that nothing but these two objects of attention, the lemon and the ringing, seemed at the moment to exist—or, more precisely, all other objects of attention seemed to *de*sist, leaving a boundless plane defined by three distinct points: 1) the lemon, seen, 2) the telephone, heard, and 3) himself, the perceiver.

When the first ring ceased, Wendell felt himself flung into a suspended but functional condition similar to the hinge-field of memory/anticipation between two frames of a motion picture. An exhilarating feeling, as if gravity had been removed. And there seemed to be an abundance of time in which to absorb the sensations of this netherworld, time enough also for a faint anxiety to erupt insofar as he could sense no guarantee of return to his usual realm; enough time (perhaps these were simultaneous impressions?) to see the inevitability of the form of the triangle, to sense that it does not need more than its points to exist (it does not require lines, the lines by virtue of the points are there without having to exist), to know that there is light in darkness the way that there is air in water; enough time to lucidly appreciate that never before had he accomplished such a quantity of cognition between two rings of a telephone.

But of course he could only *assume* the phone would ring again, then posit that it probably would, and then he found himself hoping fervently that it would. Thrill sprouted anxiety. He hoped and wished and then prayed and at last clenched his will and ordered the phone to ring. Still it did not stir. Had the first ring been a stray? But it seemed clear that the lemon—which he *saw*—was contingent upon the *sound* of the telephone for its very existence; and so was he.

Thoughts percolated within and around him, each maybe valid if isolated, but in ensemble a storm of de-ionized irrelevance. He remained aware that only two or at the most three objective seconds had elapsed since the first ring, not long enough to give reason for concern. Still, so distant did that ring seem, so far in the past; so much had happened since. Then a nano-shudder of doubt: had the phone rung a first time at all? But even if it hadn't, did that matter? Whatever the cause, he was now deeply enmeshed in a mode of nerve-wracking anticipation from which relief could be found only through the future ringing of a telephone. Might he live out the rest of his life between two real and/or imagined rings? Or would he never age, never die?

It moving slowly to the left. And why shouldn't it; the planet is rotating. My brain is RAMless compared to the All; I move at earth speed. But I have a fixed POV, do I not, what am I after all if not an independent perceiver hovering in space? And from here I see that the earth indeed moves, slowly, to the left. (But not the walls?)

When the phone did ring again—if indeed it had rung a first time, for this ring now was at best circumstantial proof of a previous ring—it seemed to Wendell such immense good fortune that for a torturous instant he kept himself from yielding to relief, lest his ears prove mistaken. He was able to determine with fair confidence that the phone was now ringing by simply listing one by one in his mind the many differences between the sound of a ringing telephone and the shape and color of a lemon. He saw that there are many differences, more than he might have under normal circumstances been able to imagine (and of course he could be reasonably sure, in fact was taking for granted for the moment that he, the perceiver, was not also the ringing telephone). Obviously under normal circumstances there is no great danger of confusing a lemon with the ringing of a telephone, a fruit with a bell-like sound, but when it's just you, a lemon, and a ringing telephone in the middle of a tantamount nowhere, similarities magnify as much as differences, and the human nervous system attunes to minor variations in a minute theme, a contextual scherzo Möbius-woven through denominators. It was the lemon (seen by him) that permitted the phone to ring, and the ringing of the telephone (heard by him) that brought into being the now fast-dissolving plane that the ringing of the telephone shared with Wendell and the lemon.

Somehow word of Wendell's condition has reached the highest floor: Hear you're having some corporeal difficulties, says CEO Greg Fuller to Wendell on a rare visit to Payroll. I can see that it's true. Still, you look recognizably of our good species. Permanent, is it?

—No sir, probably not.

—Still be a place for you here, of course. Maybe with that patch, if you keep needing it, we could waive your necktie requirement.

—Well hopefully I won't have to wear it for long.

—Can you run it through a wash or does it have to be dry-cleaned? I'm just joking, don't take it off. Let's see, your left side, that'd make it your right brain, your language center. Uh-oh! Can't lose that, can we? How 'bout it, Candice, this man sharp as ever?

—Oh absolutely, in fact—

—Deformity they say focuses the mind, maybe it all evens out. Nothing could be more important here. If there's one thing people want Fuller Communication about, it's their paychecks. A dangling modifier is something up with which you will not put, eh?

—I prefer not to.

—You read Churchill?

—No sir.

—God's memoist.

Bing! E-Michelle: A raunchier than usual something. Wendell to Michelle: My grandfathers were both sailors. She responds:

> A dirty old man from Down Under
> killed a croc and then tore it asunder.
> "For meat this will serve,"
> he said, "shoes I deserve,
> but this corpse for a condom's a wonder!"

Wendell to Michelle: Tickled.

With Wilhelm gone, there is less to absorb Wendell's attention. Escalating frequency of thoughts about his upcoming blind date leads to wondering if he might be able to steer the evening to a carnal end. A wit-born wish: he is a young man in a young man's body whose hormones have been mute for weeks—what exactly is happening to him? Mere coincidence, his assorted malfunctions? Or is perhaps this immobilized face the diseased node of a nervous system barnacled with neglected, stir-crazy sperm? Simple fornication might be a prudent short-term goal. But of course his date, a friend of friends, will expect competent conversation. Maybe with his ailment, if he winces enough, he might summon the coiled nurse in her.

But when the night arrives, the only thing he can do is dread, and by the time his door buzzer buzzes he is all twigs and wet leaves under the eye-patch. Everyone waiting in the car outside. In his fluster he knocks something from the dresser to the floor. Bends to retrieve it, stands. The after-breeze of his movement wafts toward him a hint of citrus.

He puts his nostrils to the lemon's skin. The smell pours in and fans out and up in his mind, curtains down and folds to a point of tanged secretion in the upper rear of his throat.

One day I will be dead, but tonight I hold

You once dangled from a branch, but now

He leaves the lemon to gravity, which pulls steadily through a flat surface and keeps it from rolling. Exits the apartment, puppets himself down the flights of stairs, jittery. Bill waiting in the lobby, tapping his watch. Wendell asks him if he's warned his date about his face.

She knows, Bill says; no he doesn't say she, he says her name, but Wendell forgets it before they reach the car, waits for it to come up in the introductions. It somehow doesn't. Or it does but he misses it.

He had prepped for stolid cool, but now—what is this, adrenaline? When he says to his date It's not your birthday, is it? and she says No and he says Good, I wouldn't make a very good birthday present, it doesn't sound cosmotransylvanian at all, it sounds almost ebullient, as if he might indeed make a superb birthday present. Great, now they'll think I'm downright enthusiastic. All his dour wit fouling up in the mouth of this frenetic Wendell, next to this person in the rear of this car, too small a car, why even keep a car in the city? Easy now, you're just keeping a promise. Show them you can do it. But he can't shut up.

—One of those flashes of illumination that you get once in a while when all the lines of your face I mean of your past braid together into your immediate life and you feel like you're on the brink of something momentous and all your thoughts and actions at that moment are both the culmination of and more significant than at other times and/or that your entire future life and maybe afterlife hangs on these few seconds and everything stops I mean is suddenly drenched in portent, well while I was on the admissions line on the south side of the lobby where I could see as I was waiting down that gauntlet of Grecian figures in that hallway toward the cafeteria which is a bad decision on somebody's part because they make a certain kind of person I imagine might be made self-conscious of their own slothful form as you walk down there to have lunch or maybe the idea is to discourage indulgent eating in order to keep the crowd chicly slim or maybe the cafeteria is so mobbed they figure it couldn't hurt to inspire dieting thoughts like that but now as I gaze down this hall of naked chipped white torsos they are beginning to slowly twist and face me like in a TV commercial or a chorus line or in the commercial it would underscore the product's empathy with and roots in the eternal verities of Classical culture or it would be in the musical to break out into song and they do have flutes and lyres and goat-skin drums and they do break out into song with their marble abdomens creasing like flesh and breasts and bunched nuggets flushing and cracking and rising tips of flesh reaching toward me leaking wet cement through the spreading fissures in the stone and I'm nudged from like behind, I have arrived at the admissions booth and I am expected to Pay What I Wish as always but the statues are singing:

> The number of cents you pay today
> Is the number of years you'll live to be
> So count your change in a careful way
> As now you determine your destiny . . .

In the front seat Bill and Sally are trying their best to leave him and his date the chance to become acquainted.

—I had well over a dollar in my palm but this was not a decision I could make. It shouldn't be my call, right? Gotta leave something to God.

—So what did you do?

—I put the change back in my pocket and left.

Bill turns around: Should have paid less than what your age is right now.

—It's a good thing I didn't think of that. What if I immediately regressed and perished on the spot?

—Right, says his date. Or maybe they were counting by a different calendar.

—Exactly!

They turn a corner into Holiday Season. Ogling, gurgling from the car at colored lights and happy figurines. He is informed that they are on their way to a Handel's *Messiah* sing-along. He looks down along his limbs: underdressed. His fly, though, is classily zipped.

They arrive, park, and head across the broad polished plaza leading to the concert hall. His date, whose name he still doesn't know, is sweetly trying hard to make contact, looking adrift between him and Sally/Bill. But he can't help himself. Lingers behind his companions, then catches up at the central fountain. Ooohs and aahs. All the best architects are curmudgeons. Don't you just love glass. Wendell remembering this fountain years ago, with Marge, the spray on their backs in summer. Yes, it is necessary to have time between events; life might otherwise be confusing.

They move into the hall, collect their programs, sit, wait. The musicians take their places and tune in a delicious murmuring chaos. Then someone taps a music stand and the stage goes quiet. The chorus files in, robed in blue and white, then the conductor, to applause. The lights dim. The other beautiful sound in the room, the huge crowd murmuring, fizzes to low, ceases. End of allure.

A large plastic zipping noise: his date removes from her handbag a printed score of *Messiah*. She licks a finger and flips familiarly through the heavily marked book. So they're trying to hook me up with a musician—a naive impulse. I never liked shop talk, now it's not even my shop. She offers to share the score with him, he declines, then the music begins and they are surrounded with air made orderly.

The overture passes without event. A mighty tenor sings the construction of a highway to God and requisite total destruction of Nature.

With the commencement of the first choral movement, Wendell's date, who has cleared her throat sharply several times since the whole thing began, tilts back her head a bit. Her chin lifts toward the stage, she peers down her nose, sighting the conductor, her lips part, her abdomen expands with air, and she's singing. And she looks so expertly angelic that Wendell's senses will not at first accept the fact that she is utterly tone-deaf. He has rarely heard anything like it— the dissonance is close to unfathomable, emitted as it is from a sentient being. She knows the score well, barely needs to glance at it, and the words are pronounced with utter confidence and precision, but the notes have zilch to do with Handel and her vibrato is threatening to break orbit. For a moment Wendell is as fascinated as he is horrified; but the novelty soon evaporates, and he wonders how he will endure the next hour and a half. Oh, she is self-deceived, it is painful to the ear and to the mind!

Ring a bell in the ear of a cat and it will shriek in pain. But if that cat is busy stalking a mouse, sensors attached to its eardrums will detect no movement at all when the same bell is rung. But Wendell can locate nothing to distract him. And no one else seems bothered by her singing. Monica. That's her name, why does it come to me now, maybe as an antibody. In the land of the deaf the one-eared man is pauper. He excuses himself and heads for an exit. There pops into his mind a lemon on its branch, not dangling at all but held fast at its base, the sure extension of living wood.

In a minute winter air is slapping his face out on the street, he is walking briskly, more free and light with every block. A small destiny dodged. North. And on that day man will be man and God will be God and on TV only miracles all day long. How many stations will there be? Many, but all with the same great show.

His legs are loving moving. He passes a bookstore window display, dozens of copies of *The Worst of the World*, an encyclopedia of failure with a fat beautiful lemon plunk in the middle of the word WORST on the cover where the O should be. What is *that* all about? Walks several blocks before turning into a bodega. His body heads to the fruit bins and stops in front of the fruit. His hand rises and reaches for a lemon. Twenty-three cents? Deal. Exits and walks back in the direction of the concert hall—why? Who said we were coming back? Tosses the lemon hand to hand, small lobs. The night has grown very cold and begins to flurry snow.

He reenters the auditorium fairly calm, fruit concealed, the better to not alarm ushers. This lemon is not food to me but legislation may not discriminate. Feels like he's been away for days. He takes his seat while the chorus celebrates the smashing of pottery.

—You OK? whispers Sally, her peer at him echoed by Monica's and Bill's.

—Yeah. What's the score?

He takes the lemon from his pocket and holds it in his lap. It reminds him, he supposes inevitably, of the other lemon back home. This one is a little longer, he thinks; heavier, brighter?

Monica sits quietly.

—Hey, how come you're not singing?

—I don't know this part as well.

Boy from one faith makes good, inspires a second that garbles him even as his own eschews him. For the Lord God omnipotent reigneth. The kingdom of this world is become the kingdom of our Lord, never mind the time and just look around. But why shouldn't He be subject to the laws of His own creation? You think friction exists for no reason? Even if He landed on His feet, the impact would be tremendous, bound to be some skidding. Still, better to vacuum when expecting Guests. Next time.

Oh, this glorious music! The masterpiece that kept Beethoven sane on his deathbed and prompted him to declare Handel the greatest composer of their day. Thus have art's geniuses slowed their cause's progress, pinning eternal works to fads. Oh come now. Here X, there Y.

With the final stretch of hallelujahs, Monica resumes ululation. Audience zeal froths toward eggnog thickness. Maybe God too had His youth, was a little looser with the Good Stuff. Or has just gotten Real Subtle. Waiting for us to catch up, floating around, peeping through small steamed windows. Oh look, it's my faithful servant Handel, diligent as ever, testing hallelujahs on a flotilla of harpsi-chords, crumpling splotched pages and hurling them into the fireplace, stabbing the inkwell, bearing down to forge these hot final measures. Leaps up to dance in raucous abandon, his howling laughter draws his wife into the room. *What on earth are you doing, lazy fool!* She dances him thirstily back to his stool, off with the doublet, the hoop. POV HANDEL: MRS. HANDEL clutching the blotter in her few lovely teeth, losing her struggle to hold it steady as she rides him bare-breasted as he writes, plume nib squeaking ink Toward Camera. FADE. Or did Handel prefer boys? Everyone applauding and smiling, or bowing and smiling. The fraternity of epiphany, bound for life.

The lemon floats toward him in the plaza fountain's pool; he prods it toward the center, the water gently slapping it back to bump against the wall. Light snow falling steadily, already has enpeeled the city white. The plaza occupied by post-concert dawdlers. Tinkling bells promote a group of huddled carolers, who turn out to be acquaintances of Monica. She moves to greet them, hugs and hellos. Bill and Sally introduced but Wendell remains at a distance, regroups his attention for the lemon. The absurdity of living things, of matter moving unprovoked.

Bill approaching from around the fountain, wary; stops a few feet away.

—Wendell.

—Sorry, buddy.

—Tell me the truth—are you on something?

—No.

—You really just went for a walk?

—Yeah. Look at this, it floats. All that juice and pulp and the heavy skin and it's still lighter than the water it displaces.

—You up for dessert?

—Sure.

—Are you? Will you join in or are you just going to play with that lemon all night?

—You didn't tell me she's tone-deaf.

—What? She's in law school.

—That's an excuse? Or an explanation?

—She has gusto, Wendell. If you require perfect pitch you should have told us.

—That is why I love you, Bill.

—She's terrific, but you don't know anything about her because you haven't asked her a single question about herself.

—I have.

—You're an idiot, pal.

—Well I'm not deaf anyway.

Throbbing. As if someone is tugging laterally and rhythmically on his left cheek. The lemon has drifted away some, along the fountain wall. Wendell slides to where it has caught in an eddy. Snow ridges against his thigh.

—For Christ's sake, Wend.

—She seems very amiable. Sure I'll go for coffee or whatever, if you guys want to. No karaoke, OK?

But Sally makes a show of saying she's tired, would like to call it a night. Monica lives nearby, will walk home. All their breaths visible white, moving up into downfalling snow.

—So I hear you're a student of the law, Wendell says to Monica as they shake hands good night.

He runs as fast as he can, leaping, inwardly whooping, for the subway station. Pays, enters, descends.

The receding blue-painted poles along the edge of the platform, and the yellow cautionary line (studded with rivets, lemon in close-up, pores turned outies) and filthy white station ID plaques attached to the poles, and the steel procession of girders running at intervals between Uptown and Downtown—all these lines out into space, instead of flying apart from each other into infinity, as the trajectories of stars do, as instinct seems to tell him they should do, instead they converge at the small black square of nothing that is the entrance to the subway tunnel. But tonight, looking with his one able eye, the black square dizzies into a popped reverse of itself—it boings toward him, to within an inch from his face; all the lines that lead to it seem not to recede in the distance but to advance toward and meet at himself, extended from scattered points—until the light of an incoming train washes the black square bright and sucks it back and his confused optics calm.

On the train, lemon in his lap. He looks at it and thinks again of the one at home, the one he's traveling toward. Across the aisle is a woman in a black pants suit, a French Horn case at her feet. She is holding a plump plum. Didn't know they were in season. Their glances meet. Her face crinkles slightly, an intelligent half-smile. Small wisdoms flutter between them, fruit holder to fruit holder. He winks but of course with his eye-patch it must look like just a blink. Then she raises the plum to her mouth and vigorously bites. She chews, maintaining eye-contact. Wendell can't, his eyes fall to the floor between them. The train speeds on.

He stops in at Asylum. Packed, but not a familiar face in the joint. Good. And a bar on a snowy night always feels like the center of the world. And when it's strangers all around you, then you're the center of the center. He stays awhile nursing a beer at the end of the bar, his paralyzed half to the wall. Why do they say that, the beer's nursing me. Connect the dots, Absolut to Kettle One to Bicardi to the wedges on the cutting board to the clear plastic bucket with whole ones on deck to the can of furniture polish to the Lazy Susan fragments to his own box of empty cigarettes. Oh, one left.

If the object of aerobic exercise is to increase the heartbeat by X percent for Y amount of time, hey, I can do the same by smoking one of these, how bad can the habit be? If any industry threatens to overtake tobacco, it's got to be health, so it is not inconceivable that proportionate propaganda is already long in the works to prejudice against the aerobic-weed monopoly.

People with high-stress jobs tend to have healthier hearts. Incredible but documented. Makes all the difference when cornered in a cave by a crazed bear, and not a bad sparring partner till then. Must put yourself through the ropes. Thus: dreams. Freud had it upside down. Viva adversity! And if it comes from within, why impale it on secondhand probes? The psychic equivalent of needle sharing.

—*That's ridiculous.*

—*Cherish your ignorance!*

—*What are you afraid of?*

—*We're only ourselves in the dark!*

—*Why do you draw this line between yourself and other people, it is possible you know that other persons might have ideas that relate to you.*

—*Here's to 'em. Why should I bother? Oh—knowledge is a virtue. Right.*

—*Pursuing truth—*

—*Eradicate ignorance and eradicate the self!*

—*Knowledge is food for a self.*

—*No. That shit eats us, we are the food in that relationship.*

So I never fought a bear, so what, so there are individual insects in this city who if they will be vanquished demand of me all that a wild grizzly would in hand-to-hand combat, so I can exercise my panic, I can do wrath, I can do a medley as total as any prom-night shaman, am I right, check please.

He steps out of the bar to find the snow has stopped and the city is sheer white and quiet. He has the streets to himself, ah.

At home, there it is. He plucks it from the dresser top and places it on a narrow strip of visible kitchenspace counter side by side with the bodega lemon he bought earlier in the evening.

—Yes, you are different. And one of you seems to be—mine. At least: I'd know you anywhere.

He sets it carefully aside, and with a steak-knife slices Storebought in two. Considers twin flat gleams of pulp, membrane mandalas cutting through. Asterisks. So this is where you come from. The pioneer penitentiary from Pennsylvania. New inmate is led down here, blindfolded, past all the other inmates also blindfolded. When they reach this central alcove the prisoner is spun in circles to be disoriented, then led off down one of these other membranes here.

He pries out a seed and places it in his mouth, sucks off its moss, bites through genomes for whole trees. Woody splinters.

The apartment air is thick and hot and dry. He finds a couple of old JiffyPop pans and fills them with water and leaves them on the radiators, throws open the window. Cold rushes in. I exist; I might perform actions. Climbs out onto the fire escape. The feel of snow grinding under his shoes, its crunch the only sound. Behind misty churning clouds the moon is soft and almost-full, silhouetting the snow-caked ad-hoc of TV antennas rigged by neighbors. People who sleep in a bed not ten feet from my own. Cities do thrive on walls. In between seasons, when the steam heat is silent and the air conditioners off, from here he can hear gentle snoring in wee hours.

He slides the patch up onto his forehead. The bitter wind feels good on his sweaty dumb eye. The night all white and black and stark as a woodcut. He blinks manually and sits on the snowy grating, reclines against cold bricks, lets the muscles in his face relax until he can barely tell there's anything wrong there. A good stretch of time in such repose would doubtless recuperate me. But tomorrow I will awake and go out into the world and smile and smile.

Back inside, he runs a scorching bath, eases in. The tub porcelain, brown and peeled like badly burnt Teflon, is great for his skin, a full-body Luffa. The lemon is with him. He soaps it up; then, while he's rinsing it, the little greenish brown ring at its stouter end comes off and almost gets lost in the suds. He finds it; it sticks to his finger like a contact lens. The bathwater cooling, a music of tiny soap bubbles popping by the hundreds, lemon between his knees gently bobbing. With due respect, Scylla, Charbdis, our aim is true here, cheerio. He places lemon on the rim of the tub, sets the green ring on its dorsal, unplugs the hair-packed drain, and the water begins to creep out. His body bright raw red from the heat, the lemon's yellow exuberant atop graphite-gray porcelain. No wonder Matisse was crazy for you. He dozes briefly, wakes, takes it again into his hands, places the green ring on the tub ledge. Runs cold water over the lemon, then lets it float in quickening spirals until the last of the bathwater rushes out in a long hearty suck.

Lemon teed squarely on the drain. He plucks it off the mound and sits back, it now aperch his navel. Again he sleeps, and when he wakes the room is near dark. He stands in the tub, dry and chilly, lemon clutched to his chest, leans over by the door and flips on the light, kneels to retrieve the detached green ring from the bathtub ledge. But it isn't there.

Can't find it on the floor or in the tub.

Too big to wash through the holes in the drain.

But it's nowhere.

The soul of valor but the peg-leg of passion. If passion were an issue.

The lemon sits on the beige hard drive, like himself more than half water. Remains there, not waiting but not moving, whenever he's away from his desk. He considers taking it with him, but wants to explore the curious sensation of reapproaching it from a distance, the quickening of anticipation as he nears his cubicle. He leaves and returns often. And then, late morning, after one quick lap around the floor, he comes back to find it gone. Something mushrooms in his stomach. Maybe it fell—he looks around the desk, behind the computer, on the floor, runs his hands through his pockets to make sure—

—Wendell, Scott asks. You OK?

—I thought I had a lemon but now I can't find it.

—Michelle has one.

Yes, on her desk, there it is. Michelle is on the phone but smiling at him. She holds up the lemon and points to a cup of steaming tea on her desk, then to the lemon, then back at the tea. She nods vigorously and mouths OK? and gives him a thumbs-up and continues her conversation.

—Now I can't say for sure that that's your lemon. I didn't see where she got it. Was yours about yay big, was it—

—Shut up.

Scott looks startled, then huffy. Says, Ten fingers to the lower lip, turns back to work.

Michelle hangs up the phone: Sorry, you weren't around. You mind if I use it to spice up my tea? I'll get you another when I go to lunch.

Wendell approaches her desk and stands there. It does not seem fair that he should have to explain himself. What could be more crucial to corporate sanity than the sacrosance of personal deskspace?

He says: I understand that your request is not outrageous.

—Thanks! She smiles, and as she stands her arm swings up, a white plastic knife whipping in her hand through the air; he feels the breeze on his face, flinches, moves a step backward. Her other hand holding the lemon. *Kill her.* He lunges. No, he's immobile.

She walks across the room and grabs a napkin from beside the water cooler, chatty: It's silly not to keep lemons in the kitchen on every floor, the tea bags go like mad and I'll bet most tea drinkers would love to have lemon with their tea. Or at least lemon juice [back at her desk, she sits], I mean what, whole milk, skim milk, Half-and-Half for the coffee drinkers, the least they could do [positioning the lemon on a napkin on her desk, the plastic knife finds a niche in her grip]—

—*Hey!* He snaps out of his freeze closing his hand around the lemon. He doesn't intend to stop her; he just does stop her.

She looks up, surprised.

—You know what, he says, I was kind of saving this (asks himself: Saving it?).

—Saving it? Michelle asks.

—I was gonna use it later.

—Let me just have my tea with it before it gets cold. Then I'll run down to the caf and get you another.

—No, that's OK, I mean— You know what? I'll run down and get *you* one. That way we'll both— This one I'm saving.

Backing away, he slips the lemon inside a front pants pocket; his hand stays there with it.

—You don't have to do that, Wendell.

—Yes I do. You want lemon in your tea. It was my lemon that gave you the idea. I am responsible for your desire.

—I don't need lemon, I just thought it would be nice.

—I could use the walk—

Candice's voice from immediately behind him: Is something the matter?

—Not at all—! He whirls around to face her, knocks a sheath of papers out of her arms; Sorry! They kneel together to gather the pages. Not at all, Candice. Can I get you anything from the caf?

—It's only eleven. They're closed for another half-hour.

The hum of the fluorescents gathers into a swarm and pours into his ears as he and Candice stand, gazes locked. He manages to pronounce: Closed! She clutches the papers to her chest. What were you two talking about just now? Candice's eyes cast for an explanation and her glance is snagged by something distant. Everyone follows her look out the window across the street through another window into an office where two people are locked in voracious embrace. Papers just clutched are fluttering to the floor. A leg swings out and kicks closed the door to the hall. Hands cat's cradle to buttocks. Faces mesh.

Wendell says, Do you have any lemons, Candice, or lemon juice or anything lemony that Michelle can use in her tea?

—Huh? she says, looking toward Michelle, who says, No, forget it.

Candice: Well, I think I have have some lemon bon-bons in my office, unless—

Scott: Nope, paperclips.

Michelle: That's OK, Candice, I'll be fine. Wendell, I'm fine.

Candice softly touches his arm, gestures him aside. She scrutinizes him briefly in silence, her concern faintly rippled with suspicion.

Michelle, too, is watching him, with a strange neutral intelligence.

Scott begins to whistle a Christmas carol.

—Excuse me please, Wendell says, and walks away, the looks of his coworkers hot and cold on his back.

In the elevator bank he hits both the Up and Down buttons, paces along the walls, knuckles tapping each distinct surface once: elevator door frame (outfacing, infacing), door panels, door frame (infacing, outfacing), a stretch of wall, each summons button and the panel they're set in. I have an eye in my socket and a lemon in my pocket.

PING! It's a posh sound, electronic, the doors part and standing there inside the elevator is Greg Fuller practicing his drive stroke. One hand shields his eyes from imaginary sunlight as he watches a ball sail out of the elevator and over Wendell's head; he follows the trajectory up, up, and down—and sees Wendell.

—Hello, young fellow. Say, are you all right? You look a little low on oil.

—Yes sir. Thinking about some food.

Lemon in his pocket so wet with his sweat it feels like inside-out.

—Ah, going down, then?

—No sir, actually.

—Then let us ascend together, shall we? Step in.

Wendell enters the elevator.

—*Ou allez-vous?* asks Fuller, winking.

Where are we now? Sixteen.

—Seventeen.

—Elevator for one flight, eh? I'd think a little exercise'd be a good thing for you, get some blood up into that face of yours—Fuller punches buttons and the doors close and they are alone together—but then you're probably saving it for the StairMaster.

—Uh-huh.

—Helluva memo you wrote on that tax law.

—Thank you, Mr. Fuller.

—You know by now it's Greg.

The elevator PINGs on seventeen and the doors open and Wendell exits and turns around. Fuller grins; Wendell resists the temptation to finger-sculpt his own lips into affable shape. Quick glitch on Fuller's face of something deeper than his Keep up the good work! A ten-gallon thumb up. And get some food into you! Two people enter the elevator. Tracy, Thomas, I recommend videotape. Tiger uses it. Thing about fooling with your stroke, could take years, could bring you down before . . .

Wendell takes the lemon out of his pocket. Ordinary thing. No reason not to let Michelle have it for her tea. Still. His refusal was adamant enough to make keeping its word a point of pride. Better to just ditch it. As for Michelle and the others, he can wait until the caf opens, buy another, give it to her, pretend it's this one, say its intended purpose has been canceled.

Will this seem too labored, as if he's been dwelling on the episode?

All right, forget it.

Just trash the fucker.

He walks into the receptionist's area. It is deserted. Behind and underneath the large desk is a wastebasket where he deposits the lemon without ceremony. What am I thinking, what ceremony could there be for such an act?

The primitive in him stirs, nudges: *a prayer for all deeds.*
Must expand life exquisitely, drawing the attention to every
small thing done. Do fast talkers and big thinkers and holy
persons live longer, or have that sensation? Adieu, citron.

Back in the office all seems normal, but more quiet than
normal. A static charge to the air. Straining to hear their
straining ears. COWORKER HORDES FRUIT. What next? Not
a PC stirring or even a mouse. So the lemon is thrown away.
A waste. But all right, occasionally a point must be made at
unusual expense. And what point have you made, Wendell?
Ours is not to reason what point.

The lemon deep in a wastebasket one story above,
morassed among crumpled paper and half-sucked candies—

—How's it going, Wendell?

—Oh great, Candice, thanks.

—Feel better?

—Sure.

—I'm very glad to hear it. I hate to see you distressed.

—Oh no, everything's OK. Got rid of that silly lemon.

—I think I missed something. Was it a rotten lemon?
This has gone too far.

—Yes it was, Candice.

She leaves and he returns to work.

Post-its. *What.*

The silly thing is to think that there could possibly
be anything so wrong with that lemon as to warrant
banishment. That is simply overreaction, and throwing it
out like that, on another floor, all clandestine, comes close

to superstitious behavior. If you want to throw something away, just chuck it. No need to take an elevator trip in order to expunge. What was I thinking? A fleetingly panicked mind engendered extreme and unnecessary behavior. The thing to do is to go get it and just plain throw it out, right here, in your own wastebasket. It isn't radioactive. Just take events back a little. Upgrade Abandonment to Abandon. Hell, you can even give it to Michelle after all, like you should have done in the first place. That's what you should have done, you should have returned to your desk, seen the thing missing and gone back to work without a second thought, lemons are five for a dollar, in Chinatown even six or eight. Obviously it's too late to revise every aspect of the episode, the fact will remain that everyone did observe you reluctant to part with it, that cannot be eradicated, but there's still time to square yourself with the bulk.

Quietly he slips out of his chair and out of Payroll without, he believes, attracting undue attention, and takes the elevator up to seventeen. Urgency distends the journey.

But what need is there to amend my behavior in others' eyes, to spend any energy at all on repairing: what, exactly?

Stick to your purpose. Retrieve the lemon, give it to Michelle, but tell her that it's a different one, you got it downstairs in the caf. Is it eleven-thirty yet? The clock over the reception desk unbelievably reads only twenty past. Must be off. Has so little time elapsed since those terrible—and why did you waffle anyway? Maybe Candice was wrong when she said it was only eleven, it was an informal exchange, nobody was pressing for exactness. Had she even looked at her watch? I don't think so! So it was probably only ten-thirty or so—if this clock here is right. And if this clock is right, you need to wait only twenty, or at least, say, fifteen minutes before you give the lemon to Michelle, allowing five minutes for supposably having gone downstairs to buy a second lemon. Or maybe you only need to wait ten minutes, sometimes they open a few minutes early, you can tell Michelle that's what they did. No sweat. As long as she doesn't recognize this lemon for the one you wouldn't originally give her. Is it possible? She certainly had enough time to become acquainted with it, probably anywhere from one to three minutes during your initial absence when she snatched it. Is it likely that a person would remember as unique a particular lemon casually encountered, then smell out an impostor? Should I bruise it, or otherwise alter its appearance? Or maybe there's no need to allude to the lemon as being either the original lemon or a cafeteria-bought lemon—I'll distract her a little with a note, *Thought you could use this*—yes. Something that knowingly pretends the whole thing never happened. A written wink!

Still no staff at the desk. Good: this is no time to chat or be seen. Wendell ducks around the desk and pulls out the wastebasket and reaches in—

Hey. Now this is ridiculous. You threw it out only minutes ago, it should be near the top. He reaches his hand in to touch what he sees is not there but which must be there, he fishes through clumps and wads and wet stringiness, gropes at the gossamer spare plastic bag folded at the bottom. Stolen! But who would do that? Had I been followed? Or has it been emptied? But it hadn't been overly full, had it, and the custodial staff don't make rounds until after five, or do they.

Soft bump of a restroom door closing, carpeted footsteps coming his way. Brace—for what?—how to explain? No, everything is fine, people do have reason to do such things sometimes, no shame, within your rights, nothing wrong except you forgot to roll up your sleeve when digging in the trash. Picks up and props the wastebasket on the arm of the receptionist's chair. I'm not hiding anything.

—Yo.

Unfamiliar male voice, maybe a temp whose feet enter his vision with proprietary momentum and stop. Large feet, beautifully shoed, authoritative and quite near. Wendell does not look up, he looks at the pulse in the wrist of the hand that clutchesg the chair-arm, and next to the hand a laminated floor-property tag dangling: 27. Not 17. Must have hit the wrong button. No lemon likely to be found here. Not a whole one. Not mine.

Big vague apologies. He replaces the wastebasket under the desk, dusts the chair seat with the side of his hand. The man sits, scowling, built for contact sports, looks odd stuffing himself into the small rolling chair.

Wendell commands the elevator to seventeen, which indeed clones twenty-seven in every major way. He checks the clock. Eleven twenty-three. Whatever you decide, you still have time. If that clock is right. No reason to doubt it. Underneath sits a receptionist, relaxed, regal, at home.

—Excuse me.

—And what can I do for *you*, sir?

—Do you happen to know the time?

She stage-swivels and cranes up toward the wall clock behind her: Eleven twenty-three.

—Oh, OK. You're sure it's right.

—Well, I *presume* it is. That *is* the time we run on here.

—You don't happen to have a watch.

—Do you have an ap*poin*tment, sir.

—Yes, I have an important meeting that I mustn't be late for. Or early for.

—And would that appointment be for eleven-thirty?

—Yes.

—Well, have a seat over there. Make yourself comfortable. Coffee's that way.

—No thank you, I'm fine.

—And who might you be meeting this morning? I shall dial the appropriate party.

—I'm just using this floor to prepare.

—I see. To *prepare*.

What is her name—nametag—*Uma*, could I— He leans toward her, bare eye swarthily leading, all conspiracy. Her phone rings. A wait-a-sec finger up to Wendell, she takes the call.

—Good morning, Fuller Communication.

This will be simple, this is a break. You've seen other people do such things. What one can do, another can mime. Nothing strange about the motions themselves.

Pretending the removal of gum from his mouth and the drawing of paper from his pocket, Wendell maneuvers around her desk, wrapping the gum in preparation for its disposal. He reaches for the wastebasket near her knees. Uma continues to talk on the phone as if everything were as usual, which couldn't be closer to the truth, she even leans a little to the side to allow him better access. She laughs heartily, holds the phone from her ear, shakes her head in delighted dismay.

There, topping the contents, waxing gibbous among bits of bagels and muffin remains and Styrofoam and banana peels (call *that* yellow?), and in general evincing little kinship to the other so-called edibles.

Uma doesn't miss a beat as he regains the lemon and heads toward the elevators. PING! As he enters he can hear her hang up the phone with the mandatory receptionists' goodbye: A pleasure communicating with you!

Back at his desk, he is rational and definitely within regulation. Michelle working peacefully, Scott plugging away. No need to alarm anyone, rustle up old confusions. If Michelle really wants some lemon for her tea she can go get it on her own—

Bing! There used to be a volume knob. Michelle:

Squeeze my lemon till the juice run down my leg.

She looks up at him, winks, looks back to her work.

Your Zeppelin is Hindenburg to me.

Wendell keeps the lemon in his drawer until five, then transfers it to his pocket when no one's looking.
And why would they be looking?

Ships, like gods, don't last forever; may as well vest your faith in the disproven. Haul VCR and TV to comfortable viewing altitude atop two cane chairs, reconnect, clear space on couch, pop wine, insert videotape, press buttons and twist knobs, kick back. Oops—sitting on what?

—Come here, you know you caused me some trouble today. Look, you're just in time for the show.

Pop dimple in pillow and set citrus on cushion, swig wine, splash dash on— Watch out, there's furniture under you. Rub spilled droplets into cushion with heel of hand.

When it comes to the Unsinkable, Wendell is strictly pre-Reformation, his belief secure long before Cameron appeared and nailed his 188 minutes to the big screen. What's sunk's sunk. The drowned don't sing reunion on afterlife gangplanks. Yes it is true that Romeo, had he met Ophelia, might have saved her, though perhaps not vice-versa, but press Play for hardcore history.

The wreck hasn't been seen in seventy-four years, now isn't where high-tech says it should be. For months the rickety research boat has been scouring the area with radar. The ocean liner somewhere two miles down in frozen darkness. The search team is exhausted and on edge, snapping at one another while huddled around a small black and white video monitor. A big formless something on the tiny screen. One by one but pretty quick the teammembers recognize the sunken ship, they're shouting with joy and relief, hugging and slapping backs and rummaging coolers for champagne. A great moment. Hyperspace to an on-deck ceremony where, suddenly solemn, the crew bows heads in silent remembrance of the fifteen hundred drowned, disintegrated passengers.

Passengers of what ship? Hard to know anymore. What's lost, found, is newly lost. We are gathered here today to rebury the dead and deny unnatural knowledge. We lower our eyes for the actual footage of the cold wet dregs. Fast-Forward Search, quick! Your pores are larger than mine. Black and white footage. Pause, Play: the surviving stewards Carpathia-plunked in New York Harbor. Teenagers drunk with death and celebrity smarming for the camera. Fantastic era, moving pictures as much of a novelty as sinkable unsinkables. No fixed etiquette for either. And no swarming legals. Still, the aftermath of tragedy as photogenic as ever. Slow motion, frame by frame. Caps held high over sheepish grins and stiff formal poses. The shy youngest thrust to the fore by his guffawing mates, the giddy guilt of survival sucked greedily into the lens of a rattling Bolex.

Oh, I didn't know you could swim! —No, that's Nautile, a grave-digging French submarine on a paid and praised pillage. Not you. An understandable mistake, so long-orbed and bright yellow it is, anyone would call it lemon-yellow, so deep-delving for knowledge. Now a museum display-case, relics of the French expedition: bench, bathtub, megaphone, baby shoes. I should be wearing a wreath of garlic.

Yellow yellow everywhere. In the ground and in the air. Do you have pride of color, friend? They say life in the public eye can be tough. And in your case . . . Well, what would a detractor say? Let's check the scandal sheet: bile, the blood of insects, asylum wallpaper, the nose of Hitler's favorite warhead, pus, the stain on cowards' backs and bellies, the robes of the Inquisition's designated heretics, the cloak of Judas in Medieval fresco—

Yellow press, all of it! When myopia points, look away! The red herrings of congruence have all been hatched by foolish man; they say that without oxygen in our atmosphere the sky might be yellow, but who's the oxygenator here?

It's the tie to cowardice that irks most. In that matter your color's been much maligned, at least in the West, but then there are only three primaries, and considering that blue got grief and red anger, fear is not such a bad lot, akin as it often is to excessive intelligence, eh? Tool of awareness? It's pragmatic consensus that's hued the ventriloqual herald of Caution, Slow Down, Danger. But the dominion of the sun and the lion's magnificence for starters wink of a subversion of yellow prowess. The unwieldy exertions of humans to tame yellow serve in the end as tributes to power, brilliance-doublers for a spurned source whose reflection's contorted proportions they would call shape of the clown of colors.

No, no contortions—unprecedented scope. You, tawny tot, envirile me. To whom does bare urgency turn for a cloak? In what tongue do lifejackets scream for passing planes? Bellow yellow! The skin of the great tanner itself, the face of heat, flesh of gravity!

And yellow can be mellow. In fields of corn and wheat. In India where your ancestors lent their blush to the rituals of marriage and thanksgiving. The rites of love in Russia, Egypt, China, use yellow essentially. All the gold of the earth—or is this yellow's blues? The favorite color of children, adults prefer it least. Edenophobia a real world problem. Not something Bosch suffered from in his skies, or Turner in the harbor, or Giotto in haloes or Lascaux in caves—or Van Gogh in *L'Arlesienne*, remember? She looks to have been posed in front of a lemon, or inside one; but Vincent had a general weakness, called yellow a color to charm God, used more yellows than all his reds, greens, and blues combined; he wrote of building toward yellow with supporting colors, preparing the canvas for its entrance. And still some call it the emblem of his illness. It is true your spectrum's as hard to resist as the sturdiest virus. Kandinsky declared that lemon yellow hurts the eye "as does a prolonged and shrill bugle note the ear"—and named his only opera *The Yellow Sound*.

But, particulus, do not let me simplify you, you are no monochrome. Here is a limy green blush and snowy crater where you once joined your stem. Its antipode, your end, your lately flowering end, your nipple, you are ever so slightly green, there in your dappled aureole, extra acid, there. One side creased where the tip bends in, just the smallest bit more deeply cool, more pure glacial yellow. Every pore darker than the surrounding skin, and wherever you have been scratched or scraped you are brown. "Yellow." What is yellow? Not even or no less than an Impressionist's sleight of light, the mating in my eye of green and red, a hovering in the air between us, phantom child of flesh suggestion and mentis reply.

Wendell's eyes are closed. The silhouette of lemon on his retinas sinks into the living black of his lids. Something in his brain tilts and travels in a syrupy wave.

He opens his eyes and sees his shadowy reflection in the television screen, production credits falling like snow.

I am speaking to something I hold in my lap.

You have a lemon in your lap. You are talking to a lemon. It is an it.

A lemon is a lemon is a lemon. Cut by humans into slices or wedges, placed or squeezed into many foods and drinks, it will enhance flavor in a universally prized manner and is often the featured ingredient itself:

Squares, hot toddy, hollandaise
Marinade, curd and mayonnaise
Scones, meringue, meat braise, brandy
Marmalade, humus, grog and shandy.

Peel minus pith equals zest. The zest is cherished by all humanity for its store of lemon oil and its ornamental value. For instance, spiraled down the side of a glass, the zest is an attractive enhancement to the serving of almost any beverage. DNA tests show that termites are a distinct species and never evolved from cockroaches, but fungus and humans are close kin.

—*Granita, sir?*
—*Yes, a double.*
Open a book.
—*Gremolata?*
—*Perhaps later.*
Read. Something tranquil.
—*Over your caviar?*
The poet's shelves.
—*Imari?*
—*No, Tuscan.*
—*Just lie back, darlin'.*

For some, books make a hearth. For others they are a cumbersome nuisance made moot by the virtual world. Sit with Thoreau under a gentle reading lamp. Or just this bare lightbulb. Read the calm words of a thoughtful soul:

Shall I not have intelligence with the earth?
Am I not partly leaves and vegetable mold myself?

The path of a tear down a lemon's slope is difficult to describe. Stretch a string between two points along its path and you will have yourself a useless map.

The shape somewhat changed? Not quite as spherical as once?

The truer the map, the less practical it is. Better love your map.

This is my life, I am free to—free to what, and what for? Make some tea and squeeze you into the tea? Pile you by the dozen in silver porringers, strategically posed and pricked to liberate your bracing aroma; grab you when I need to soothe my cough/whiten my shirt/polish my window/shine my wood/tauten my skin/gentle my tap-water/dry my beer/brighten my copper/sympathize my ink/neutralize my alkali poisoning? What is that thing they do, slice the bottoms flat so you can stand, the world's finest chefs—

You know what you could do if you wanted to is just get rid of the lemon, you really could. You can always go buy another. Destroy it. Take a bath and play Titanic, which broke in half as it sunk.

Tear it in two? Leave it to the lemon sharks?

They are the most highly evolved of all sharks.

Try to keep things in perspective, because this is what we want, I mean I do.

The air in a space shapes itself around the center of that space.

Pop!

Pip, Pulp, Peel.

Poop.

Pop!   *(etc.)*

Somewhere there is a telephone, all these buttons to choose from—

—[phone is fumbled] . . . Hello?

Tapenade.

—What? Who is this?

—Bill, I need a favor.

—Right now?

—Please.

—What is it?

—Can I come over?

—What time is it?

—For you it will be nothing.

Buttons everywhere! Knobs and dials and switches. If you touch the world with wisdom you can turn off the VCR and TV. Cool. Throws on his coat and leaves the apartment and gets halfway to the stairs before realizing: he's left it behind.

The forgettory is working, fantastic sign. O welcome, sweet denial.

Breathing a little easier, he returns to the apartment and retrieves the lemon, forces himself to move more slowly.

A taxi is yellow but looks nothing like a lemon inside. LIFE IS TOO SHORT TO COMPARISON SHOP. Printed on a sticker on the separating glass, and in smaller print: SUPPORT SMALL BUSINESSES! Wendell rolls down the window and breathes in the pumpernickel night. This is you, Wendell, yourself, Your Self, it is yours, now grab ahold.

He knocks on the door but produces no sound, knocks harder. Hears shuffling slippers. A dot of light flares the peephole. Bill groggy-voiced behind sliding deadbolts. A jerk and a squeak. His face in the crack.

—Sorry, man.

—It's cool, but Jesus. Bill lets him in, relocks the door, leans back against it, arms in a bathrobe crossing.

—Friendship's greater duty: to refrain from imposing or to allow the imposition?

—Skip it, it's late.

Wendell takes the lemon from his jacket pocket, lets it hang in his hand at his side.

Bill nods toward it. Another one?

—The same one. I wondered if I could get you to demolish it.

—You know we love you, Wend, but after the other night, Monica called to ask why we hadn't warned her about your fetish. We didn't know what to tell her.

—If you could just step on it or cut it in half or throw it out the window.

—Looks like a perfectly good lemon, man.

—I'm sure it's a tremendous lemon, I just have no use for it.

—So what's the big deal? We'll refrigerate it.

—You have to kill it.

—Kill?

—Well, wreck it. Crush it, you know.

Bill watches Wendell pace the linoleum.

Sally comes in, towelling wet hair.

—Hey Sal. They hug. Sorry to wake you.

—Not me, him.

Bill sighs, flips a switch. A bluish tube of counterlight flicks on humming. He digs in the silverware drawer, withdraws a large steak knife.

—Will this do?

—Wow. That's really serrated.

—Sal, you want the honors?

—What honors, says Sally.

—We need to annihilate a piece of fruit. Bill hands her the lemon, proffers the knife handle.

—Slices?

—Slices OK, Wend?

—Maybe not with that knife?

—Wendell, says Sally softly, is this that lemon from the other night?

—Actually, no.

Bill: You just told me it's the same one.

—No, I had another one at home that night—this one. The other one I just bought because . . . you know.

Wendell stands still in the middle of the kitchen watching his feet. He can sense Bill and Sally's glances join, then separate back to him.

—Here, says Bill. He holds the knife handle out toward Wendell, who takes it gingerly into his hand.

Tiny teeth.

—And the lemon, Sally says. Wendell takes it from her outstretched palm.

—Well gee. OK. I don't know.

—Wait! Sally rummages through cabinets. Bill, you know that zester your mother gave you?

—What?

—When you moved in here, she gave you a whole bunch of kitchen stuff— Here it is, and she sets on the counter what looks like a cross between can opener and crossbow.

—Have you ever used one? Bill asks her.

—You use it to take the peel off, she says. In a spiral.

—It looks medieval, says Wendell. I was hoping for something a little more pedestrian.

—Well, we have other knives.

—OK.

—Maybe a butter knife? Would that be better?

—A dull blade? Wendell asks, doubtful.

The three of them stand in the kitchen and think. Wilhelm patters in and winds through their legs, his back arched in gregarious pleasure. Human crisis makes good catnip. Bill kneels to grab a box of dry catfood from under the sink, shakes some into a plastic bowl. He makes kissing sounds at the cat, who noses the food lazily, leaves the room.

—Maybe the thing to do is, I should just forget it. I'll take it home with me, as if it were an ordinary lemon, which it is, and I'll keep it in the fridge until it rots like everything else.

—What is it, Wendell, says Sally, that has got you so worked up?

—I'm not so worked up, do I seem so worked up?

His friends steer him into the living room and sit him down on the couch, and sit on either side of him. Someone turns the television on, keeps it muted on a news broadcast. Wendell is talking about the lemon's color, its weight, how good it smells, the fact that it exists at all. Are emotions just chemicals in the brain? Bill reminds him of old times, when they were out every night tag-teaming wit on women all over town. Not with this kind of talk, pal. Wendell asks them if he can sleep on the sofa for the night. They say sure, Bill adding, You both can.

Wendell sees Sally look sharply at Bill, disapproving.

—I just need to be with some people.

—Sure you do, Wend.

—Maybe you should take a few days off.

—I really am sorry about the other night, guys, my behavior.

Bill and Sally are quick with assurance, no no, it was fine, Monica liked him a lot anyway.

—Right, says Wendell. I uh . . . I thought up this thing
on the way over here:

> 99 lemons up there on the wall
> 99 lemons up there
> I've got one on my shelf
> Take one for yourself
> 98 lemons up there on the wall

—I'll go get you a blanket.
—I think I'm gonna crash.
The room twitched.

Wendell falls asleep on Bill and Sally's couch, for how long he
doesn't know; when he awakens the night is still very dark,
very quiet. But in the darkness he sees as never before. No
longer a sticky insect flailing in the mad web of his own
cognition, he is a soaring surveyor of his mind's terrain in all
its patterned glory. An integrated luminescence of meaning
and purpose, spun on the loom of his essential being, this
mind belongs to him. He can see as distinct all that it is and
all that it is not. So many why's laid bare. His whole life
has followed and still follows this form; what adheres to
it is effortless, yielding reward, and all that resists brings
confusion. The madness of this very evening, his exertions to
be true to what an irrelevant ethic would deem dictum:
unnecessary. The architecture before him is all he needs to
know. And should he ever misplace this clarity, he can regain

it, he sees, by yielding to the next evident simplicity: the clarion fist of now. Shoulds and doubts are moot moths flitting through the chambers of living mind, drawn to light but by light made hysterical, fodder for tumbleweed.

I am lucid. The will from within is vivid. Good friends and hosts, I regret having alarmed you unnecessarily, having publically dithered with regard to what is now a burning resolve.

Wendell neatly folds the blanket, dresses, pockets the lemon, and lets himself quietly out of the apartment.

There once was a race of giants, lemons tall as redwoods. We know exactly their size and form, for men built shelters for them. Or crucibles; the precise original function of these buildings has been rendered oblique by time. But the magnificent chambers still stand, long since adapted to substitute uses, and they count among the most inspired architecture on earth. From the Haga Sophia to the Taj Mahal to Florence Cathedral to St. Basil's, on and on and on. Some nations were host to great broods of lemons, indeed the wholes of Islamic and Russian architecture seem lemon-bred, albeit from a strain whose shape has long been extinct, with shoulders, a thorny crown, and a waist. Or are those gobbed containers the burnished stylizations of memory?

For the most part, the great lemons appear to have borne a direct anatomical connection to you, and the grand scale of their traces help me to map your smaller parts, to see them and to name them. Your pedicel, that uppermost tip of nipple that springs flowers where you touch the sky, architects have enpoemed this in the lantern and cupola of their glorious domes—the hoods, or second skins, of the Leviamons. Many of these buildings agree on a cross to evoke the flower that was once there, and these are often made inaccurately from gold—or perhaps the vanished race did erupt in petals of gold, in trio. The Parthenon was ingenious toward the flowers, with its circular opening at the spot for sky-peeping, for greeting rain and sun.

Where have the great lemons gone to, leaving their crusts strewn like gargantuan cicada shells across the hosting earth? And from where had they come? Was it a Leviamon thrown or fallen from beyond this world that sent up the sunproof dust-shroud that did in the dinosaurs? Giants have a way of falling, lemon. Size is not everything in the mad scrimmage of evolution.

But the great lemons live on in the architecture of man. Our own country boasts a generous share of neo-Leviamoniums, especially in the city and state capitol buildings across the continent, even downtown in this city. Bruno Taut's Glass House of 1914, that structural clarion call for our era, was a perfect hemi-lemon. Lately the form has been toyed with like everything else. Wright's Guggenheim looks gourmet-carved, and the Bilbao stepped on—nothing dome-nostalgic there, it may be the most citrically correct building of our time.

Or does this honor fall to the opera house in Sydney, that honest sideways stack of peels?

Eye to eye in the morning sun. Cougar, doe, stone pharaoh. I take you half-warm from my sleeping calf, into the cup of my hands, lay you upon my chest. You have a front, you have a rear—two different types of end, two beginnings. Nipple Nose. Dimple Butt. Look, we've both come from somewhere. Let's let navels nuzzle.

No, a falling lemon *can't* have extincted the dinosaurs. Dinosaurs we now know were warm-blooded. Frogs survived—all of them. If anybody was going to die from want of sun, it was frogs.

Are *you* my lemon? Flat like a sunfish, juicy with a stiletto tang? No, you're Lisbon.

Are *you* my lemon? Thick-skinned and big as a grapefruit, easy prey to frost? No, you're Ponderosa.

Are *you* my lemon? Hedge-friendly, virus-prone, a little on the sweet side, popular in Europe for centuries, not brought to the Americas until 1908 when plant explorer Frank N. Meyer encountered you in Peking? No, you're Meyer.

Are *you* my lemon? The juiciest, most popular, most cultivated of all citrus? An aristocrat's susceptibility to cold and insects, and, provided with an ocean view, a year-round bloomer? Yes! You, good pod, *you* are my lemon.

You are Eureka.

You understand that heaven and earth came into being for our sakes, by definition: simply because we exist.

Or is vice-versa closer? Both of us slaves on Planet Bacteria, me in the boiler room, you wafting cool?

Coffee is brought by a woman who says, Can I do anything with that for ya? Her look is dull, illegible.

—What do you mean, "do anything"?

—Want it sliced?

Wendell looks at her levelly. No I don't.

—Whatever.

Many eggs due before him any moment now. He feels acidic, armed against cholesterol. Mind if I call you *le monde?* Bouncing lemon very lightly on the porcelain. Just an ordinary person waiting for his breakfast, happens to have along with him le monde.

Lemming, lo mein, new loam, la nom

—You two together?

Whirls around on his stool, sees it is the hostess greeting customers at the door. He regrets his sudden reaction and swivels, ultra cool, back to his coffee. Yes, we are. Lay low, my loan, knell Om. Live your life. Drink this coffee black.

But then someone does address him, nudges his elbow while settling on the adjacent stool, patchside, Wendell has to turn to the left a bit to see the kind-looking old man, who says, Good morning, his face fluttering with a nervous something. Says, Hate to use an old saw, but it does fit the situation.

Wendell nods crisp assent.

—Sunlight, a gentle breeze and whatnot. The man's finger wags, slows to a point. Voice dropping to a private hush. You got something going on with that lemon, don't you.

—What do you mean.

—Yes indeed.

—Just a lemon.

—Of course it is. And what's-it-called is just another whatchamacallit.

—I don't know what you're talking about.

—Documents. Listen to me. Photographs. You hear? Necessary means. As the magazine determined, "The Search for Adam and Eve," the original, the cover story, the first human being was a black woman. They figured she was big, like a building, maybe.

Wendell signals for more coffee.

—If I ask you to pick me up a copy of this article, can you find it? Is it under the counter, even? Eve, evening, darkness, this is what the facts are, but not in the history books. The church in Venice, there are four sculptures on one side of the building and each of these statues' noses? Broken. You mean to tell me this is a coincidence? The little pinkies are in perfect condition, but no noses? Can't hide the lips though, difficult to kidnap just lips. You have kids?

—No.

—Plan to?

With quiet gestures Wendell tries to make plain to everyone in the diner that this conversation is being forced upon him. His hand finds the lemon and closes around it. Fellow eaters, clearly it is evident—

—Red bellies and black bellies rubbing in the night. Yellow bellies and white bellies. Pesticide, friend, kills bugs, sure, but—

—Thank you *very* much, Wendell says to the counterlady as she sets his breakfast down in front of him.

—You know the side effects?

—The what? And to the counterlady: Some ketchup? She slides it to him.

—I say, the side effects?

—I get you gentlemen anything else?

The man's attention is locked on him, so Wendell must answer for them both. Not right now, thank you.

—Renders crops mute and passive. Keeps fruit and vegetables in their place. "What, that old cucumber say something?" "Nah, that's a stupid ol' vegetable, just give another squirta Chanel Number 77." All this will come out eventually, truth has a way of squeaking through, but in the meantime you take good care to establish yourselves in the record. Knew a fellow in the service, very attached to a jar of strawberry jam. Sent by his lady, I'll be waiting for you in the strawberry patch, this type of thing, one red berry to another, what have you. Guy carried this jar everywhere, 'long with this note that went: BURY ME WITH THE BERRIES, in case he got ix-nayed, which he did no problem, and for Christ's good sake do you think his buddies listened to a measly note? They scarfed that jam before his body was in the damn bag. Sugar on the battlefield, talk about sweetness.

The man stirs his coffee with a fork, sets the fork down. Wendell has stopped eating. His mouth has gone a little dry. He catches himself; looks again to his food. The man leans to sip his coffee without picking it up. He slurps loudly, then tilts up his coffee mustache face at Wendell, says: Don't let that happen to you.

Mozart kept a starling for a pet, who would sing back to him his works in progress. In a notebook Mozart gleefully reports the bird's having changed the sharps to flats in a melody from his Piano Concerto in G—and what a glorious difference it made, *Das war schon!* When the starling died, Mozart was griefstruck, and held a graveside vigil with poems and hymns.

Wendell combs the Web at work. Curious, but without conviction, he rummages in Fetishes, and a few clicks beyond Animals and Knees finds "Stomping": naked people who jump up and down on fruit vigorously, and do other things to fruit. A celebration of fruit and sexuality. Hm. What say you, shape? schwa? critical mass? Always a place for you on me hard drive.

He looks to his left across the room and out the window and sees again to his dismay the towering billboard that grew over the weekend, with its spaceship-sized lemon wedge obscuring his favorite strip of sky. The lemon is of credible yellow, and sits in a puddle of juice ostensibly its own. But the wedge is entirely, undeniably intact, its membrane inviolate: impossible. Such blatant ignorance looming above the dense crowds of midtown is frightening. Lemons do not yield juice until squeezed or otherwise exercised. The rest of the ad (for a liquor), while stylized for graphic effectiveness, appears reasonable enough in color and perspective. Then what's with the puddle? Apart from the patent physical absurdity, the spent juice would seem to undermine the wedge's potential value as a drink accessory.

Bing! E-mail. Michelle: You know you have a brightness control knob along the base of your unit. The stompers. He clicks fast, turns around, mouths thanks, she winks.

The most prominent lemon in the city is a lie! A propagation of one of the worst myths surrounding lemons—that of the ever-juicing, self-sacrificing citrus, the Obsequious Orb. But any lemon neutrally observed will virtually glow with august dignity. Placed proximate to even the most skillfully mixed drink or exquisite seafood, the lemon will wait until squeezed before yielding its juice, and, having secreted, will bear the marks of additional concavity, creased hide, droplets on the rind. The latent lemon is all elegance in its arid veil, and, squeezed, begs no airbrush.

He looks at his own. True, it has browned some, maybe more so than most city fruit. Few have the opportunity. But surely it is not far enough gone to warrant Scott's speculation that it might pose some sort of health hazard to the office.

For God's sake, it looks alive, Wendell. Fungus, guy. That's fungus. No, you kindle my cubicle still. Even from the shadowed corner of the hard drive—which is out of sight of everyone else's eyelines—so Scott must have deliberately come around for a peek—

First of all, the pale green circular splotch with the white outward edge is plainly not lemon itself. The disfigurement is clinging *to* lemon; even if it has somehow penetrated into the interior, there is no reason to consider that it is *of* lemon. So Scott's language is inaccurate. Nor is the encroaching brown cloudiness in any way native, the fuzzy darkness that began at each of the ends and moves inward a little every day to shadow more and more of the yellow—that is not lemon either. It will be futile to explain this to Scott, who evidently sees only what he wishes to.

In places, when he looks very closely, he can see that the brown areas are spotted with tiny wan blisters, little volcanoes that rise even further than the mossy green from the yellow surface. The nipple has become more pronounced—due to a general dehydration that has the lemon looking longish, almost figlike—and its nub is entirely brown (except for a pinprick of beige at the very tip, a vestige of flower stem), while the aureole is caked with the same white stuff that crests the spreading green. And there—another, smaller verdant island. Cenozoic, in all; a blurry ensemble of continents.

Wendell carries the lemon into the Xerox room, where there is a sink in which he sets it (when he puts the lemon down on any flat surface, it rolls a tiny bit until its next discrete facet squarely meets the plane beneath, upon which it quickly secures a balance and comes to rest). Pours dishwashing detergent over it and then cold water (hot has recently been cut off to all floors beneath the fortieth, a budgetary measure). Scrubs vigorously with paper towels, dries it off.

Now it feels more uniform to his fingertips, more like its old self, but all he's done for its acned complexion is flatten it into lithographic unity. The greens are slightly thinned in places, but this has only revealed a somehow even stranger orange just underneath, at the splotch centers. The larger of the two green patches resembles a reptilian eye. Wendell presses in on the ends to approximate former sphericity.

Back at his desk, he waits for the right moment, sniffing lemon in the meanwhile. Recently its smell has been partly eclipsed by a deeper note of acid, oxidation, a vegetative odor— Canals, neighbor? Too straight for Nature—proof of Intelligence! Whoops, mine.

Office metabolism at a steady calm buzz. Candice near. No one on the phone. OK.

Wendell removes the snapshot of Marge from the wall and tears it in half loudly enough to attract everyone's attention. While slowly ripping it into smaller and smaller pieces, he announces, with direct looks into his coworkers' eyes: This lemon here on my desk is to remind me that the person you see falling to the floor in tiny bits was no good. In relation to me. Defective.

—About time, Scott says. Michelle grinning big and straight at him. Candice clears her throat: I am sure I speak for all of us when I say that I am very, *very* proud of you.

I think, I act, I achieve— *Bing!* Dear God. Michelle. Scusi, papilla. He clicks.

> There once was a lemon named Wendell
> When you squeezed him he bellowed like Grendel
> A monster he was
> All covered with fuzz
> His pees a blend worthy of Mendel.

A cigarette, I think.

Elevator to the ground, past Bucky in the lobby—

> But we're not just our animal natures, are we; one allows for a certain degree of mental or spiritual evolution, and certainly language we agree inhabits this sphere, so to say I do this or thus because it is my *nature* to do so is to ignore half the story. We are so civilized as a species. [laughter] But Nurture after all is a trickledown child of Nature—can we agree on this? Vice-versa is a question, I've never much cared for the chicken/egg argument, silly thing's probably deterred many a fine mind from science; maybe there's a spin-cycle but it looks as if Nature's the propelling weight—there may even be no Nurture in the wash at all . . .

In such a great mood, so lemony swimming in thoughts, he boards the subway and sees a bright joy of yellow on a purple ribbon—helium balloon floating free in the car. The air from the ceiling vents steadily pushes it downward so that it appears to hover, never actually touching the roof but rather bobbing its way from the far end of the car straight toward him. All passengers are watching, charmed, moving out of the way to let the specter pass.

Wendell snatches the balloon by its ribbon on his way off the train, heads up and out onto the street. Waiting for his cue. It comes in the happy shriek of a child chased in play, the slap of running sneakers. Wendell relaxes his grasp on the ribbon and the balloon shoots up into the sky to become quickly a speck visible for minutes as it rise up and east, over buildings, river, swallowed into air.

Freak spring dusk, rife with footfalls of joggers, squeaking of stroller wheels. Toss and catch in the park along the river. You go up, you come down. Looking very Fauve today. Pigeons gather as if expecting bread.

Who is the earth
and who is the moon, here?
Who circles who
when there is no third?
Pocked and porous and small, true;
yet you are my all, no mere;
and I am the pale one,
always falling toward you.

Speak to me of flying.

—I will. I will tell you a story.

I was a mere sprout, maybe five. I knew, as do many children, that the simple reason human beings do not just flap their arms and fly is a collective self-delusion that we cannot; I, as yet unspoiled by the deceit, would be able to fly.

One day I donned a red beach-towel cape, cleared an area in the living room, and notified my folks of my maiden flight. My dad went into town to buy film and my mother made iced-tea and my father returned and loaded his instamatic and together they rearranged the furniture to give me extra room. My mother took the phone off the hook, her custom at special moments, and I stood on the arm of the couch and waited for my father to turn on an extra light, this was before film got really fast, before digital, you wouldn't remember, or do you remember far past that, I'll bet you do, I'll bet Eden was one giant camera obscura.

I memorized my flight plan, but just in case pathed it out with marbles along the floor: I was going to circle the living room three times to become familiar with my new skill, then glide through the dining room and into the kitchen and open the refrigerator and grab myself some ice-cream from the top freezer, which normally I couldn't reach without dragging over a chair. Everything was set.

Wendell sits on a bench, places lemon down beside him. You look good on green, but that's only natural. He moves it a little closer to his hip. On the bench slats it looks like a whole note on the staff. Here, put this leaf here. Now you're a fermata. Musical notation in three-dimensions: an improvement. Leave nothing to the conductors.

Almost dark. The air cooling. The skyline of the city a symmetrical hill, tippytop slope mirroring bedrock depth.

—My folks still have the photograph. I'm completely horizontal in the air, my arms outstretched, stark naked except for this bath towel twisting out behind me. You can see our two cats sitting on the couch behind me, curled up together, and my mother's foot in a sandal in the right lower foreground. And me in the air with this expression of absolute terror! A kid's nightmare panic look.

Then one second later he was on the floor with skin burns from the shag carpet and excruciatingly painful bruises from the marbles on his shins. Both his parents laughing. The ice-cubes in their drinks rattling, a squealing siren noise from the phone receiver stuffed under couch cushions. Marbles still rolling, hushed over the carpet, brittle and loud across linoleum.

—I should never have let them watch me. I'm sure my intuition was correct—I could have done it, I could have flown all the way to the refrigerator and hovered there eating ice-cream at a grownup's altitude. But Heisenberg prevailed; that event was completely, irretrievably altered by my folks' observation of it. They had to have been watching me with at the very least a gentle condescension— how could they not, since no one in the history of the world had ever flown bare-assed before. Icarus, no model. No matter how lovingly they looked at me, their thoughts bombed me out of the air.

Now stay just like that . . . very nice . . . almost finished here, just touching up your nether portside . . . You see how well the upside-down question marks work for a rounded low left? Not many humans know how to coax them from the keyboard, a multi-key operation that must be performed in entirety for each one. Notice how the point-size decreases as we near the light source. The illumination here is typical Rembrandt, forty-five degrees/single source from above. Remember this light from your orchard? You would have had it twice a day. But you know who you'd really dig is Vermeer. A symphonist of yellow, the color infuses all his work—

From across the office, Candice: Who are you talking to? (Wendell starts; was he speaking aloud?) Is that my memo?

A quick click and the answer is yes.

Candice comes near, scans the half-finished memo, an important one for All Employees with a credited cc to Fuller.

—You know what E. B. White said about commas, Candice? They should fall like knives in a circus act.

—E. B. White? From Earth, Wind, and Fire?

—I don't know, maybe.

—Yes I saw them live once. Like a circus, certainly. Well let me know when you're finished.

—Sure.

To the point!

That's you.

Model back from break.

Click.

Now, Vermeer knew singularity. Where most painters in his day, in order to evoke three dimensions in two, directed their lines of sight to vanishing points outside the frame, Vermeer's perspective tunnels inward. Like a lemon in cross-section, all membranes heading toward the placenta.

What humility he must have had, ay? To honor with every stroke the core from which his world grew, and resist the vogue efforts to outguess Nature at her own game (which he did anyhow, in spite of himself). Click. Please be informed that all employees who have not switched to Direct Deposit are herewith requested to do so. Click. Proust saw the lemon in Vermeer, and almost died from a stroke that hit him as he stood rapt before the smallest daub of the master's yellow: *His giddiness increased; he fixed his eyes, like a child upon a yellow butterfly . . . "That is how I ought to have written . . ."* Click. Direct Deposit is a quick, convenient, and efficient means of receiving your salary. When I hear of such things, click, I almost dare believe we are not alone, click, For more information, please contact the Payroll Department. Click. Look at you! Click. Candice, where are you— Shall I print it?

—No, don't bother, I'll read it here, and she is next to him again, peering at the screen. Wendell, what is this?

FROM: CYCLOPS
TO: KRYPTON

You wobble when you roll,
the toggle of your tickle
such a buoyant shade of fickle
it's a wonder you are whole.
Do you never pause to wrinkle?
To mull, to muse, to crinkle?
One might think you have no goal!

—Oh, sorry.
Click.
—Thank you.
Oops.
Memo approved. Ten minutes later a master printout is sent to Repro, and the next morning at 9:00 A.M. there is a copy on every desk in the company. All that tree spent. Should really begin using e-mail exclusively for these things.

Wendell's phone rings at 9:03. Early for a call. Early for me to be here! Wherefrom all this juice, holon?

It's Candice, sounding stiff. See me in my office.

Be right back, jot.

Wendell and Candice face each other across her desk, not speaking. He does not know why he's been summoned, why the door is closed, why Candice has instructed Scott that they are not to be disturbed.

She is uncomfortable, she doesn't know where to start. Wendell points to an eight-inch silver rod studded with a row of rhinestone lights and mounted on a black onyx base, sitting on her desk. If Liberace had a metronome.

—There is that clock that I love so much.

He pulls the rod to one side and lets go. A spring tugs it back and it moves very quickly side to side, its little studs lighting up in a perfect choreography that reveals a digital image of the time in the air, which evaporates as the fanned radius folds to still. A conversation piece, usually. Candice looks at the rod, the time gone out of it. Sighs. Looks out the window and back at Wendell. She slides a manila folder over the desk toward herself, opens it, takes out a sheet of paper, passes it to him: a copy of his latest memo.

—Is something wrong with it?

—Read it.

He does, remembering Candice's hand-clasp of delight, yesterday, after she'd inspected it on the screen.

—It's good, no?

—Look at the bottom. The cc.

He looks. And sees what should be Company President and CEO Fuller's name, but is not quite.

Not at all.

In fact—

He croaks: Wow.

—Right, says Candice.

—I don't know what to say.

—Neither did I.

—K and L are so close to each other on the keyboard. That's bad design.

Candice laughs with a strange part of her throat: Well, what can you do?

—Has Fuller seen this?

—He's the one who called me.

—Of all places for a typo.

—Are you sure it was a typo?

—Of course. What do you mean, does he think—

—Well, he's very upset. He's, um, lashing out. Wendell, don't you have that system that underlines misspelled words in red? Because this word should have been underlined, I looked in the dictionary.

—Sometimes the computer is wrong. I mean—

—Maybe you should—

—I don't mean—

—Because—

—Of course I should.

—Well . . . I'm sure he'll eventually calm down. A person doesn't become a person like that unless he learns to control his temper. Right?

—Candice, I am so sorry about this.

Her lips flutter silently. She rolls back in her chair, mulls the air for an instant, stands. She paces to the window and turns, perching on the sill. Eyes on the carpet in front of her. Says: You haven't been yourself lately, have you? I've noticed, you know, I do pay attention. Recently your sentences haven't been as . . . She looks up at him, strains for a smile to encourage.

—Fluffy?

—Is everything OK with you?

—Sure.

—Really?

—Of course, why?

Gently: What about the lemon, Wendell.

—What lemon?

—Wendell.

—If it's all right with you, I'd like to take a few minutes and write Mr. Fuller a note of apology, I'll double-proofread it, of course.

—No, he wants to see you in person. He wanted you to go upstairs immediately, I persuaded him to wait an hour. He was so emotional.

Wendell gives the time-stick another flick. So this is my chance to make a run for it.

—That's your decision.

Back to his desk. Scott stops by to tell him a joke. Once there was this bartender, very strong hands, he could squeeze a lemon dry, regulars used to bet on him, some new dude would come in, skeptical, out to impress, bets would be placed, bartender would squeeze and squeeze and hand the lemon to the new guy, guy would squeeze, not a drop left ever, the guy is legendary among weightlifters, boxers, longshoremen, no juice left for any of them after the bartender squeezes. One day this scrawny dude comes in, bets are placed, bartender does his thing, squeezes some lemon dry as a rock, hands it to the nerd, nerd real casual squirts a steady healthy stream of juice right out of that lemon down the bar right into a shotglass. Unheard of! What's going on? Total havoc! What the hell? Answer: Nerd's from the IRS. Get it? Wendell, you get it?

—Yeah, I'm not—not right now, Scott.

Fuller's fingers are pressed into a steeple, his eyes like storm clouds behind. Wendell stands in the doorway. The older man snaps into a sudden Welcome! Come on in. Freaky wide smile, good teeth.

Moving slowly toward him, Wendell apologizes for the typo.

—Please, please. I'm well aware the greatest writers of all time were usually too drunk to spell their own name, let alone that of their chief executive officer. Not that I think you need any loosening up. Not that I don't think such an error could have its origin in the spelling of even a mediocre scribe. I was a little riled at first, true. But it seems to have been put into perspective.

—I'm glad to hear that, sir.

In the broad-windowed sky behind Fuller, cumuli part to let through the sun, silhouetting him in stark light. But the wind is quick, the clouds come together, the light softens. Then flares again.

—Sit down.

Wendell sits. And sinks.

—That's a water chair. So's this, but I prefer mine firm. Fuller watches Wendell's face, each feature. How's that paralysis?

—I'm getting by, thank you.

—I hear you've been re-bachelored. That can be tough.

—I'm surprised you know about it.

—Been feeling all right?

—Well it's turned out for the best, I think.

—Has it? From what I hear, things've gone a little sour.

Fuller leans forward, gripping the corners of his desk. He favors complex-patterned ties; the knot of the one he now wears bunches up under the ball of his chin and sits there like a gargoyle.

—What's all this I hear about you and a lemon.

Wendell imagines Candice on speakerphone to Fuller: *He's been under stress lately.*

—I don't think it's relevant to work, Greg.

—Interesting thought, that.

—It's a personal matter.

—Wendell. May I ask you. Have love and work become so estranged in your mind?

—There are certain things—

—The lemon has been in the building, has it not?

—There have been thousands of lemons in the building.

—But we're not talking about thousands of lemons.

—More than four billion each year are consumed in the States alone, sir.

—We're talking, correct me if I'm wrong, about one single particular lemon.

—That's five pounds per capita per annum.

Fuller exhales. He pulls out a side drawer in his desk, reaches in, takes out an apple, closes the drawer, places the apple on the desk between them.

Wendell looks at the apple, then at Fuller, who continues: Now it so happens that I don't eat apples, or in fact eat any fruit or vegetables at all. I follow a dietary routine developed and first implemented by my great-grand-uncle [without taking his eyes off Wendell, he raises an arm and points to the wall at a framed photograph of Buckminster Fuller], who early in life ascertained he had no time for unnecessaries. Fruit and vegetables comprise a relatively early link in the food chain, being consumed by animals which we humans in turn consume. Bucky decided there was no reason to eat food that others could eat for him. He ate, exclusively, top-of-the-line brisket of beef three times a day for fifty years and died happy, lucid, and productive at dare I say a ripe old age.

Fuller picks up the apple and leans back in his chair, spins the fruit like a globe between two fingers. He places the apple on the desk again, next to a plastic geodesic-dome paperweight. Pats each with affection.

Wendell says: Like Renfield.

—Eh?

—Dracula's servant, sir? First he ate only flies, then he fed the flies to spiders, then he fed the spiders to rats, which he fed then—

—Bucky did all right by meat.

—He sounds like a fascinating gentleman.

—Perhaps you are wondering: What could the great polygenius Buckminster Fuller possibly have to do with me?

—Well—

—By "me" I mean you. I no longer eat apples.

—That's probably smart, unless you get the organic ones, all that herbicide, pesticide—

—But if I did. I would take the apple into my hands. I would salivate in anticipation. I would lower my jaw, thereby parting my lips, and I would tear into the fruit with my teeth; I have excellent teeth. I remember the flesh of apples from my youth, and I know how good they can be to chew for those who have the time. I would masticate. I'd crush the pulp, suck the juice, I would swallow and digest and expel.

—Your right as an American omnivore, sir.

—It is my prerogative should I choose to exercise it. And why would I not. Do you see anything unnatural in such behavior?

—Of course not.

—Such foods hold for the human many delights. I remember apples. I remember lemons. At one time I regularly tasted lemons fresh-picked from the top orchards of the world. Oft was the hour I enjoyed the company of a lemon—in drinks, sprinkled over a filet of this fish or that, spread throughout a lovely slice of cake. So I would like you to feel that I am not entirely removed from you by way of our respective experiences. Perhaps we might even consider ourselves equals in some way.

—Greg, I completely respect whatever role you choose for any food in your life.

—Wendell, in the halls and so forth "Greg" is fine, but in the privacy of my office I'd prefer you entertain the perks of surnamity.

—Yes sir.

—"Fuller." As in: Fuller Communication. As in: Fuller Communication Company. Wendell. Here we are together on a planet in a room. We are alive, each of us, in the workplace, right now. You are in my life, I am in your life—the same life you share with that lemon of yours. The sun is shining over all of us together.

—Sir, I'm listening, I appreciate your insight, but I wonder if I might assure you the lemon has nothing to do with my work for this company—

—But that is precisely my point! Why should we draw lines where Mother Nature and Father Time do not? Shouldn't you feel comfortable discussing what's on your mind, sharing the contents of that very heart upon whose beating depends the writing of important Fuller Communication memorandums? When your lady friend left you, you took a personal day, did you not?

—Half a day.

—Still it is evident how work and what you call "personal matters" are related, grant me this. You crave a languid Thursday afternoon holed up in some turnpike motel with that lemon of yours, there's more to consider than simply your raw lust. You have to think about how the event interfaces with the rest of your existence, do you not?

—I don't know what they've been telling you about me and my lemon, but I can assure you it is nothing like what you seem to think. It is a purely Platonic ownership. It doesn't interfere with my work habits or with the quality of my work. As a matter of fact, since I found it—

—What do you take me for? Do you think I think a typographical faux pas of Richter-scale intensity happens because the mind wanders off onto some anonymous, nugatory foodstuff? You took my name, and of it obscenity rendered. That was either a deliberate act of malice—which between ourselves I do not think it was—or it was the footprint of attention slinking from its post to drink from sweet and secret waters. And I want to know the name of those waters and whether they are salt or fresh or lapping at my door or are in fact tar pits so I can warn others not to go there. I want to know if they are contaminated with something terrible so I can quarantine anyone who's been slurping there . . .

Wendell looks out the window, down onto the street far below where a bright confetti of umbrellas opens at once. But he sees no rain, hears none. And the sun is shining bright.

On the desk is a silver mug, its engraved inscription facing him: FOR THE FIRST TIME IN THE HISTORY OF HUMANITY, IT IS EVIDENT THAT THERE IS ENOUGH OF THE FUNDAMENTAL METABOLIC AND MECHANICAL ENERGY SUSTENANCE FOR EVERYBODY TO SURVIVE AT THE HIGHEST LIVING STANDARDS.

—and where I come from, Wendell, it makes no difference what you read on the label, it's what the stuff in the jar tastes like that matters.

Wendell says, his voice very low, The mistake was unintentional, sir.

—We have so many different kinds of people working here, all manner of deviant, I mean that in the most technical sense, they are thriving in all departments, but this thing with that thing of yours, I frankly don't know. A lemon, in and of itself, is benign enough. But so is plutonium in most contexts. Gender, race, religion, so much is protected by law, insured by good sense; disability; every variety of interhuman behavior—

—Sir—

—so many, many things. But I'm afraid that if we open our doors to this, we open them to just about anything. By which I mean, well, it's precisely because I am not sure exactly what I might mean that I'm so concerned, Wendell. Just before you arrived here in my office, I looked up "prejudice" in the dictionary. Permit me.

Fuller opens a well-thumbed desk dictionary to a page-marker tassel. Reads. *Prejudice: discrimination against an individual for an attribute or attributes associated with a group of which that individual is a part.* Closes the book. But in your case, Wendell, what is the group? I want you to know that I don't stand in judgment.

Asylum is empty and quiet in midafternoon, unfamiliar. Doesn't recognize the bartender, pleasing as he's in no mood for chitchat. In a corner out of the sun he watches the smoke from his cigarette rise and disperse; impossible to do this at night when the air is one collective puff.

The lemon is stuffed deep in his pocket.

He is no longer welcome on the premises of what is now his former job. His last act of duty: to delete all his files. Candice with tears in her eyes, Scott a surprisingly compassionate handshake, Michelle something in a sealed envelope.

He sips Scotch, new for him. Must seek advancement where I can. Tries to think his smoke into shapes, but they all turn out elliptical. His palsied mouth can pucker only a squashed circle. The jukebox belts too eagerly for the hour.

Everything is a blind tug-of-war. You enlist a machine to produce a particular letter from the alphabet, but all the others loom as imminent possibilities. Of course you wouldn't prefer to be at the office at the moment, per se. But why, finally, have you been canned?

Scotch tastes foul, delicious. History to deem tobacco as twisted as slavery? The sun sets and the place starts to fill up, turn into itself. When Nort arrives for his shift, Wendell moves with his drink to the bar.

—Here early.

—Well yeah.

—Alone today?

—Nah.

—Where is the little sucker?

—It lost me my job.

—No shit.

—Right.

Nort looks down toward Wendell's drink. Wendell does too, sees his own finger merrily stirring the Scotch. Can he stop it from stirring? Yes. Can he will it to his lips? Now: bite! Next time a candle flame for you.

Then again, who knows. For I have seen, through the viewfinder of a thermosensitive weapon, the human heart in all its senseless splendor, I have heard its thundering in digital quadrasound. The heart is not a loony mess of gloopy flaps and percolating snailations, it is a lively gob of joyful leaping-forward/diving-back. More glossy than matte, it is all of a piece, break-dancing master of the house, the liveliest spot in the body. My so-called misshapen heart valve. A diagnosis broken-toed in ancient rubble. Get with it: the heart begins as a tube in the womb, it's an ud-cum-castanet.

Bill arrives, says, sitting down: Gentlemen, I have news. A round for us all. He sees Wendell's state, looks at Nort, who explains. Bill earnestly tries to make sense of it. Wendell replies: Fuller called me a citrussexual. Do you think that's what I am?

—Citrussexual? says Nort, refreshing his Scotch. That's pretty good.

—He says since I'm the only one he's ever heard of, firing me is not "discrimination" on his part, not a thing of principle. He said that my presence would eventually take a toll on the equanimity of my fellow employees.

—Listen, Bill says, I think you can contest this.

—You are new to drink this evening.

—Why'd you bring the thing to work?

—It's always with me.

—Where is it now?

—I got it.

—Christ. You do know that you two are weird to behold.

—Of course.

—Do you talk to it?

—It doesn't talk back.

—Has the thing supplanted your interest in women?

—Would you please address yourself to my visible eye?

—Sex.

—I am not impotent. And stop saying "thing." Forget it. Isn't it all like a newsprint photo. Stand back far enough and it makes good sense. Get too close, just haywire dots. But closer, inside just one dot, and it all goes pure, beautiful.

—How's Sal?

—She's great. We—

—Now there's a normal thing, you two. Congrats, man.

—Nort, hit me.

—Sure man.

Three matchbooks, one with three matches and little grip, one with no matches and a grip that eats a match before he knows it's rainsoaked; two matches wasted and another wasting what's left of the grip on the first book, uh-oh—but: third book's full and dry. Why do I do this?

—What's with the cigarettes, Wendell?

—Instant addiction upon unprecedented impulse purchase. Say nothing. I have a television.

—No you don't.

—I know what it's doing to me.

—You like the color of the box.

—I do.

Bill sips his new beer. Wendell switches malt count, says: Buckminster Fuller said the government should give every adult a million dollars, that out of those hundreds of millions of millionaires one or two ideas would emerge that would pay for everybody.

—Wendell.

—Yes, Bill.

—Tell me.

—Of course.

—Your life is rich, full.

—Hey Bill, can I ask?

—What.

—Yeah, with you guys, you and yours.

—Sally?

—Right.

—Your friend Sally.

—Yes. Can I ask you?

—What are you asking me.

—I'm asking you a question.

—I don't think so.

—You're having dinner. Haven't seen each other all day. There you are. So. Now. Wendell implores with his hands.

—Wendell, what are you talking about?

—The two of you sitting there. (my little glass is very deep, stomach please my drink do keep) You talk. You have conversations. I assume too much?

—Did you and Marge talk?

—I can't remember, William! I will be a sonofabitch if I can recall. We must have said things to each other every night. God knows what they were. But I can reconstruct. An amusing incident at the workplace. Crazy dude on the subway. Your hearts' desires. Events in the news. You go to a movie. You come out of the movie, I loved that actor, didn't you. Wasn't it funny when this happened, I thought it odd that XYZ was there, didn't so-and-so remind you of what's-her-face, wasn't she better in, what about that other flick, wasn't that great, when did you know that guy was the guy.

Bill touts twaddle. Content isn't everything. Empathy. The glow of togetherness. The music of speech. The little thoughts are the thoughts that bind.

Wendell hears himself speak as if from several stools down, watches the man with the eye-patch talking about ways of cooking an egg; one person says poached, another person thinks poached, each's idea the jet trail of unique nature and experience. Sense imported is sense domestic and only seems otherwise because human beings are lazy, scared, self-conscious beasts who use less than nine percent of their brains and make up the difference by leeching off the minds of others, nobody coming individually wrapped like fine chocolates but as mixed nuts, a shame because each is a species prototype: on the hardwire level a problem solver with a fail-safe mechanism for making problems. The knack to see that *Such-and-such is suchwise* in the undulating field that is the world is no better than the skill to make a snapshot of a star, the which, to sail by, is insane. Well some do, I guess. *This is thus! Thus is that! Hup, hup!* Every recipe is a family recipe.

The man with the eye-patch and lopsided face wobbles on his stool like a tired top, raises his glass in a toast: To the champagne and caviar of company! To friends and acquaintances! A deaf and dumb hermit could write the news accurately, but why waste guano? He declares his companion a board, a totem, a living tool of fear and suspicion. Who seems to be shrinking away, but then so does the entire bar. O the pompous pity of the self-appointed sane, the proud sober. I am trying to uphold a standard. Tell me, says Bill, and his lips form the perfect portal of a word, the exact contour of a particular abhorrent circumference, and his vocal chords leap to the supply, and his tongue is ready at the dock and flicks and casts out this word that Wendell has never asked to know, a terrorist word in the ears and heart of little Wendell all through his formative years, Bill intones this word with great gravity, the cumulative weight of usage of this word for generation after generation, weight under which Wendell has nearly been crushed and that seems to still be heavy in the near sky at all times, and to which Wendell hopes to add and fears adding his own weight; and the sundry modern pilot-fish of this prehistoric shark of a word tickle and gum him as the great word feasts; and Wendell's spilled blood draws other words, words that have swum centuries seeking this very bar tonight. And hovering in the air just above Bill's head is a cartoon devil perched on a leather-backed chair that floats in a cloud of blackness, a splotch of some sunless cranny in a specialist's library, red leather, brass rivets, dark polished wood with the initials of dead lovers deep-engraved with the blade-points of knives with bejeweled handles, ceremonial blades, instruments of measurement, a chair donated in memoriam with a bronze plaque with his own surname etched in ornate slopes. *I have seen photographs of this chair!* Bill pronounces the word that Wendell cannot see or hear without teetering fundamentally, Bill draws out the complex, full-bodied syllables and weaves in the air connections between things that do not exist. A magnificent soufflé of reason. Psychology so subtle it begs Uzi fire. Tell somebody something and it always flies back in your face. Completely irrelevant!

Wendell's body tending upward off the barstool. He summons gravity, settles. Nort musing aloud about surgeons whose sense of touch is transmitted to the tip of a scalpel, wonders if something similar is going on with lemon, an infusion of charisma.

—I know it is a lemon, Wendell explains with large patience for the fifty thousandth time in one second. I doubt supremely that it feels, nor do I attribute to it any out-of-the-ordinary sentience or iconic power. But we must hold to the tissue, the *issue*: cobwebs in the air, an endless nebula of Being Together. Because a person is just a sieve of the world, they cannot be any more than what they know, and every person knows too much to be coherent. I remember conversations, sure I do, I mean I forget every word but I remember back-and-forth, I remember my net gain, net *game*, the horrible feeling—hives on my days! And you better face it, you better face your truth, man. If you don't face your truth you develop a muscle of falsehood, and this muscle gets bigger and bigger until it is so powerful that you can't be honest with yourself about anything, you can't maneuver and you can't see anything clearly anymore, and your life is a wreck. And the human ego will do *anything* to conceal an unpleasant truth from itself, and the psyche is a slithering den of collaborators. So what now is this very cold, twisted sort of sideways look you're giving me, it does not appear to be very genial. Note: Never pump a friend too hard for the truth. A schooner lists in the wind. He's so smug, my best pal. But I do not say out loud that he and his in their mutual exchange of data over an infinitely limited gaping chasm of meaningful meaninglessness, that they are this or that; I do not explain that there is only one reason for the fact of people existing in the first place, and do you know what that is? To hit another human is an act of raw insanity, which I do not have in spades. Bill up and asking for his check, the two of them so smug, tilting back and forth, their little covert nods, handshake, but I do not yield, I surrender no secrets, *Pay the bill and sally forth*, I am not blabbing aloud, I am not yelling, demanding a response, poking a fellow's chest, it is futile to yell through this roaring ferocious surf-sound. Who inhales from the wrong end of a cigarette, swallows hot ash that dribbles and burns all down my throat? The whole bar careens, spilling Bill out the door, there are strangers turning toward me, hello you seem like well-intentioned people with interesting things to say but the fact is I miss all of it because I am must-notting, must not vomit, I am pure lurch and lunge via stools what and chairs and knees and whose shoulders huh on my way to the back of the bar to the bathroom to the bright lights, whoops, ahhh, slaloming tiles, where I stay, it's a magic carpet, I stay for a long, long time.

Wakes up walking before dawn, the city and sky silent spangles, hint of moisture in cool air, his head a dull scratch, wolfing a packet of aspirin, a paper pint of orange tipping juice onto his wrist as he stumbles to avoid a skittering rat, eye-patch down over his nose, dripping orange juice. A Hammety hour, steam rising through pavement here and there. On the corner Gloria is pointing her cane in fury at a broken pay phone. *Don't you be tellin' me I never consider myself welcome, I BETTER be welcome and it's YOU who don't call. I call you up, you answer the phone, you tell me you can't talk, your baby's screamin'? I never told you to go and have kids, I would never tell you that.*

Wendell passes, croaks Gloria, make nice, regrets immediately his singsong tone, which Gloria may mistake for ridicule, and yes she whirls on him, cane shaking and thrusting, eyes wild. *What's it to you, fucker?* He knows not to take it personally; in this mood she probably doesn't even recognize him.

But then she says: *Don't nobody who sleeps with tomatoes be tellin' me how to speak to my family.*

—What did you say?

—*I SAID NOBODY FUCKS A TOMATO GONNA BOSS ME, don't make no difference you got no damn TIE on, walkin' around like some stupid Timbuktu.* But then the anger drains from her face, she averts her eyes like a shy child. Quivering, the tip of her cane lowers slowly to the ground. She leans heavily on it for support, cocks her chin forward. Softly, adorably: *Where's that tomato, lemme see that thing.*

—Where did you hear this about me and a tomato?

—*Come on let me SEE*—she stomps, shrieks in pain—*You see what you made me do man you live in the damn CITY don't you KNOW that? Probably don't even close the window shade when you do it. Edwin told me all about it said you sleep with it at night buyin' MILKshakes for it. Whole block's TALKIN' about you, kissy-kissy. Get your autograph on the wall actin' all debutante? That what you want? Free eggrolls? Shit, my FOOT!*

—Gloria, all it is, is, I have a lemon. Where the hell is it. Not a tomato. Here.

He shows it to her, holds it out on his palm.

—*Not so close, I don't wanna TOUCH it, Jesus Harold Christ.* She peers very closely. *A lemon,* she says sweetly, awed. *I knew it was somethin' crazy.* Then a scholarly frown: *Don't look fucked. Look fucked UP. Like YOU.*

—No it doesn't.

—OH YES IT DOES YOU DON'T BE TELLIN' ME WHAT I SEE WITH MY TWO EYES YOU PERVERT—

—Shhhh, Gloria—

—Probably do it ten times a day, right? So who's on top?

She is gleeful, cackles and swings her cane up straight at Wendell's face; he has to jump back to protect his exposed eye.

—THIS MAN SLEEPS WITH TOMATOES! THIS STUPID SONOFABITCH FUCKS A TOMATO!!!!

Wendell snaps to and trots home without bidding her good morning. Lemon and an open day await. Fill each with the other.

—Pervert.

III

Irked by zilch, burden bare,
We are a bliss of patience.
Floating at the doting pace,
buoyed by bubbles in lazy eddies,
we stretch and twiddle
and further the druther between us,
slowing time in a dam of kisses.

No she, no he
no far as I see any sex
unless there be some taciplex
to better limn you, fruit;
if so, it's not yet news to me,
thus moot.

No flab, no gab
no ciferated babbly lovey
chummy this and that, no shovey
kissy huff and puffin'
(the futile fence against the drab)
just one long sweet nuffin'.

Good, stay, shine.
Or should I say: reflect.
I'll speak to you of astronauts
and what they did collect.

On the moon was found a rock
that seemed to have been set there
by a hand that never clock
or compass helped to get there.

It told them more, that moonstone,
than a jabbermile of earth;
in snowy whitely quiet tones
it spoke of planet birth.

Of the labor of the sun it sang,
of gravity, her firm umbilical.
Back home, in fun the NASA gang
did hang upon the garrulous crag

a name: Genesis Rock.
Apt, don't you think?
From the well of such lore,
it is good for us to drink.

Calcite, that day, cuz,
specced what the moon was,
but there are many informers in our midst
spilling the beans of the mother stalk,
seeing nothing necessary is lost
on the journey from then to then.
Carbon consistent, amber unambivalent

endlessly talk; helixes whip and clamber
that the musts shall be preserved.
Marvelous messengers teeming
in sentry through topsoil, lacing
radioactive sheets of rhythm in space:
fable, chlorophyll, ostinado—
word gets around.

And so, over the shoulder of time,
keen eyes have cribbed our cladogram rhyme . . .

Before a point did fine the gall
to undertake an overhaul,
self-interrupt to self-befall
in farflung flaming free-for-all,
we were everyway equals.
And when the boom did spread its shawl
and scratch and yawn and scrape and mall
the flesh of virgin space,
it didn't change things, not at all,
not between us.

Words slow into stars, scab into earth

Soils lie still under barren air
under unceasing starlight

The earth rotates upon its moors,
makes seas unseen crash on deaf shores.
Ammonia, methane, hydrogen, water,
mother stuff, no son or daughter;
twelve-hundred-million-year-old tit,

warm, round, fecund, yet unbit.
Soft explosions, bingo-ball motions,
still no life in all the oceans.

And then there was our jagged father,
sky-sprung root come to prove
a dame fertile; light and earth mated
in their salty bed, flashed and shocked
in furious conception the sleepy elements
bolt-awake: birth so immediate
it seemed to seed its own possibility.

In warm shallow seas the children lay,
single-celled souls (still aswarm today)
churning wisps of womb-memory
into froth of savory air,
which in a quarter billion circled suns
filled and floated jellyfish tons,
an aquatic groove that found happiness
(*feels good*)
could have stayed just like that
(*oooh that feels good, keep driftin'*)
could have gone on like that forever
and almost did and would have, too,
'cept this prehistoric jam-crasher
you know the type,
blowin' out of his element
spoilin' everything for everybody—

For me and you
it was a coup, no question,
when an accidental pocket in a seaplant grew

and seized our lofty bastion
of mutual regard.
When that weirdly bubbled being
though it had no sense for seeing
was left by tide on land
it must have somehow took the view
and known it for grand;
the sun made this plant dry
and it didn't die: our general root.

Twixt then and now,
post-first pasture, pre-first cow,
the world was lesser damp.
Under the hides of mousy fur wearers
(lemon-size milkers, my own prebearers)
four-chamber hearts pumped quick
and constant blood, fueling climb and scamp
and the birth of clonish young.

This biofrenzy smooching soil
flicked and stirred and sucked and flung
dirt hazard into shapes of flowers,
bright frocked fronds of fertile dowers
clocked with a frolic of mammals:
seedhappy suitors, lovers, looters
feting, unwittingly begetting
innumerable species of arbor.
Shoving roots, guzzling sun,
chloroplastic Jujitsu flipping
carbon monoxide into oxygen, chopping
noxious exhale into sweet air.

(While two of my kind vie for breath
and two of yours for soil,
one of each make a peaceful cross-pair;
your aesthetics make sense of my kinetics.)

The clan of the Ruticae sour,
oddly known as Rue,
Order: Sapindale plants that flower;
such is citrus, so are you.

First squeezed by hands so small and brown
it seemed the beans you fell upon
(lentils, heart of diet)
were sheddings of the skin
of the squeezing Indian,
who also knew to tease you
to a tea to quiet quease,
to set the pulse and mood at ease;
they wooed you well, good lemon.

When Romans blew through
neighborhoods that knew you
they took you for the signature of the sun,
which you were:
the brightest thing they'd seen
since they crossed the Mediterranean.

Scattering seed, their greatest skill,
newing need through wanton will,
stuffing orchards into sacks,
they set out on an inadvertent mission.

By route and roam through Africa
to Egypt and a new homeland,
where, pulped with light and life,
gold-pith'd and rinded in sand, you joined
the stanzas of the poems of the gods;
bananas, pomegranates, figs—
you basketed with bigwigs
in this life and the next,
through the randiest rooms
and the dandiest tombs
of the digs of the Valley of Kings.

Westward you continued,
in Sicily and Crete grew so gloriously sweet
you thought you'd never leave;
but by and by, Helen of trees,
you were come for,
drafted to a stench war at Versailles
where life, glazed to near extinction,
stank to high distinction.
Who better to brush the walls
of gilded halls, and fresh air defend,
than you, fragrant friend?

But alas to public purpose
you were soon a private prize
when idle nostrils passing
flared 'neath hungry jaded eyes.
No less than the King's right arm
was sent in huffy haste to charm
please, some restraint from bold court ladies

who'd discovered lemons plucked and kissed
wondrously reddened lips—
and oh, the sweet breath sucked from pips!

(Was it in Lou's kitchens frilled
that your leaves first wrapped fish grilled,
their oils moistening, evenly relaying
hotness of flames?)

In Andalusia loving Moors
set your roots through castle floors
from where you canopied the doors,
nostalgic for the northern shores
of Motherland.

Then with Columbus on his tours,
usurping lime on every ship
(your juice the worse to scurvy),
enough of you survived the trip
to open New World branches.
Cortez himself soon strolled among
your leaves in gardens walled,
conquistadorical considerations
sprouting in citric shade:
fresh carte-blanches.

For size you rivaled melons
in the South; eyes out West
dazzled to your hue's bright best,
and it is there, in Pacific loam,
as if to strut the deep joy of true
roots in a long-sought home,
you bless with your bloom all seasons.

Or maybe it's a Higher Zeal
that fuses California peel,
tawny pilgrims having lodged
in the heart of a Frisco friar
who based the very crux of his creed
on what he believed was the Good Word real.
He spread your seed in claim and deed
all up and down that coast;
holding you high, he'd shout his highest toast—
May your soul smell fresh as a lemon!
—and raptly of your many virtues gush.
Might he have seen to century nineteen,
and from the future an inkling fetched
of native lemon value stretched
in the C-starved canteen of the Gold Rush?

Eureka!

Wendell seems to remember something Bill said to him at Asylum, before they stopped speaking that night and maybe forever. *To an Onanist, fetishism must seem a high social art.* But I am no tree-lover twisted toward a portion. If I am a fetishist, so are all monogamists.

Oh, it's pettiness, the gist is of another order entirely, because in that very space you occupy, what was there before? You, unseen, unseeable? Nothing more true or astounding. What does this mean, what does this make you?

Commotion in the neighborhood. Movie set or fire. At the art store two blocks from his apartment there is no Lemon Yellow in acrylic, which the salesperson explains is the best all-surface paint. Wendell settles on Cadmium, a little harsh, but time and bustle will surely mellow it. At home he clears a space on the floor and spreads a mat of newspaper, gets the white plastic carving board from behind the sink, and the kitchen stiletto he washed earlier. The decision was made last night; he will remain firm. Don't think about it, you know what's best. After all, two weeks is your normal refrigerated life span, you've lasted much longer than that already. Quintessence intact. You are no lemon but an egg, the democracy of molecules says so. You are a dream or the fruit of a dream or the root of a dream. You are no lemon but an orbish yellowness in a room, next to a knife, mapped in my eyes. You are a theorem, I prove you by my own congruence. There is chaos in the data, we're complicated entities, but our elements make us kin. Knowledge is our nature, love our due.

Wendell collects the rest of his equipment and assembles it neatly on the newspaper. He sits, cross-legged, inhales once deeply, and with a single neat longitudinal slice, splits the lemon open.

This I have never done with another.

The lemon's dryness makes the skin tougher to cut than ripe skin, but the incision is straight and clean from nub of nipple to stem crater. A Tupperware bowl, rinsed and dried, catches the juice, which he squeezes out first with one hand, then the other. Not the quantity of a fresh lemon, but what juice there is has distilled into a citrus essence that flares his nostrils and sears his throat like cold wind, forcing his lungs to expand, leaves him breathless.

He puckers open the skin. Two fingers scoop out the pulp and pips, which he lets fall into the bowl, joining the juice. O, that is you in there. A seed falls onto the newspaper. He picks it up and places it in the plastic bowl. He runs one finger along the inside wall, feeling for any loose pulp or membrane that may remain (some, yes, stringy). A burning at his cuticle. Citric acid kills sperm, in Third World countries half a lemon is used like a modern diaphragm. Wendell sucks his finger and tastes for the first time in months the sour cry of this juice.

His arousal is as powerful as it is sudden, he is compelled to free himself from his clothes to avoid the quickening pain. He ripens and blooms like a timelapse flower, the lemon peel all sun and wind and rain, wilding to envelop his flesh and catch his mind, the whole act lasting only seconds. His primary after-feeling is of lucid strength, as if it has been his own cavity scraped free of unnecessaries and filled with life-force.

He sets the lemon down on the newspaper, careful not to spill its new contents, and crumples a stray page into a loose bunch, a protruding corner of which he inserts into the peel. The paper begins to absorb the viscous wetness, and Wendell gently pushes, little by little, the entire ball into the lemon, all the while pinching and pulling the skin until it has filled out close to its original shape. Pressing the slit closed with one hand, he uses the other to suture by running doublestick Scotch tape in circles around the fruit. A spiraling mummyish wrap from bottom to top. Holding the sticky fruit at its ends between his thumb and forefinger, he dips it into a bowl of sea salt, rotating until evenly covered. He sets it down again, squeezes out some Cadmium alongside it, and pulls off the tiny plastic silo from around the bristles of a brand-new paintbrush.

All goes well. The rough veneer of salt seizes the paint, and immediately mimics the leathered pores of an ordinary lemon. While the paint is still sticky, he sprinkles paprika for visual texture here and there, why not a fillip of cinnamon, and when it dries he is happy to see that a second coat, which might undo the salt's effect, will not be required. A bit glossy, true, but the cadmium is overall just fine. The surface imperfections caused by the folds and buckles of tape work beautifully for verisimilitude, and an hour later the extra sheen of skin like glazed ceramic is the only extremely noticeable deviation. A full-figure double bell parabola. Weight and volume normal. Topography intact.

Hello.

And as for you, ex-innards, enjoy your stay in Plastic, heart of Freezer County, gets mighty icy this time'a year, but there's room for ya.

> As a flower drops its petals
> one by one through minutes, hours,
> so shed you the pulp and rind
> of earthen sours.

Wendell washes and dresses in sweatclothes and climbs out onto the fire escape into the rich smells of many dinners cooking. Backs of buildings loom tall and gray and darkening white. The shadows are stark, but the sunlight where it falls is warm, a beautiful evening. He sits on the sill, lets the cold shoot through him. A bluejay hops to a thin black rail not ten feet away, is quickly joined by its mate; rare birds in the city, even in summer, and it's not yet spring. Wendell flips up his eye-patch to see more, enjoys the feel of his eye drying in the cold, blinks by hand to lubricate it. There is a weightiness in the air, as if the sky is about to burst, not with rain but with colors, or singing, or some ancient invisible truth. The air is multitudinous, in the throes of ripeness, and his senses, tautened to full stretch, overlap at their extremes like the tops of trees. The thrum of a low nearing airplane erupts briefly into sight as it passes between buildings; the bluejays fly off toward the plane as if to greet it. Dolphins of memory break a surface with their backs, expectations, childhood sensations, enchantments of still, solitary minutes before meals, the simple knowledge that certain entities, known, dreamed of, exist.

Wendell breathes deep. He begins to perform an exercise shown him by his doctor, designed to rally dull facial nerves back into action. All the vowel sounds mimed in turn to extreme, a conjugated Om.

Inside again, he picks up the tube of remaining cadmium yellow and makes a line drawing of lemon, straight from the tube onto the homogenous background of newspaper stock quotes—

Who's there? A clicking and receding. You do not attack me because I do not fear you. Otherwise undecided, you will only bite if I think you might. When I notice you, I become you, and you sense in my weakness the terrain of your advance.

= = =

Yes, you are shiny, and reflex convexly. The world shimmers in your enhanced slopes. How much more like a lemon you were before; how much less so then than you are now!

—Yeah, and butterfly garnish. Thin slice tied in the middle with a sprig of parsley.

—No kidding.

—Then there's the Horse's Neck, peel hangs like a mane out the side of the glass.

—I'll have one of those.

—On the usual?

—Please.

—I understand what you're saying. You are making sense grammatically. But then you always have. In that way you take after your mother. Yet I would caution you against equating evolution with progress.

Wendell is facing his parents over the remains of a half-eaten dinner. Everything was fine until midway through when his mother asked about the lemon, which he'd set without ceremony on the table at the beginning of the meal. He's tried to say as little as possible. And now his mother tells him, not for the first time in this conversation, Stop joking.

—I'm not joking.

His father: Was this happening while you were with Marge?

—Not that I'm aware of. I hadn't found it yet.

—It, his mother hisses. Her face tightens one more notch, then cracks into loose wet grief. She burrows into a napkin.

—So this excludes other relationships?

—I'm here talking to you.

—Do you consider yourself celibate?

—That's not a simple question.

His father's grimace redoubles. His mother's eyes are wide and wet over her napkin. His father: What's not simple? Do you. Have sexual behavior. With it?

—*Of course he does.*

—The relationship, if that's the word you're comfortable with, has been consummated, says Wendell. But I don't consider sex to be central to it.

—My God, says his mother.

—It's more than that, I mean.

—What would you have us tell people?

—I don't care, Dad. You seem to have little difficulty euphemizing other parts of my life.

—I never heard of such a thing. His father rises from the table, begins to collect dishes. You have no idea what you're getting into. Carries the dishes out of the room.

—Do you talk to it? whispers his mother.

From the kitchen: Of course he talks to it!

—Yes I do. But not condescendingly. Not like to a dog.

—Does it talk back to you?

—Mom, it's a lemon.

—Is it a talking lemon?

—It speaks yes in a way to me, but not out loud. I'm not insane.

—I'm praying.

—Lemons don't have lips.

—But they have a mind?

—Please.

—My God.

—It doesn't—

—Does it have a name?

—It's a lemon, Mom.

There is the wind that rolls you around the world, and there is the equal and opposite wind that keeps you right where you are. We live in privileged times.

Wendell's father reenters with a carton of chocolate milk and a jar of baby gherkins. Perhaps the kitchen has inspired him to philosophic detachment, for he resumes his seat and muses: At least he saves in birth control. Then looks at Wendell: If you ever used it. You always liked lemon foods a lot, eh? Am I right? He always liked lemons.

—No more than anyone, says his mother.

Wendell says: I read somewhere that the rise of the mirrors as a commercial industry, etiquette, and standing armies, these all emerged together.

—I see. And today is the anniversary?

—Around 1500 this happened.

His father clears his throat. So. Where did you two meet?

When did I know you were in the world? Distinct from all else and even so: of the world? Did I know you first as a colorful thing, or had I heard you tumbling down a staircase and did I turn to see you fall, and then I never would forget you and I wanted to be near you and I touched you, my hands closed around you and I held you, our two skins were touching, a child and a lemon in their natural relation; I would have smelled you then, and probably would have put my tongue on your skin, you would have seemed big, like a melon to me now, maybe I even saw you then, saw you and then stopped seeing you, and now years later—

—Dad, if you could. I try not to talk to the lemon as if it were a person. If you could try to remember.

—Ah. No illusions.

—It's a piece of fruit.

—You talk *to* it like a person but you won't talk *about* it like a person.

—We didn't "meet."

—Then you bought it somewhere, where?

—Country Table? his mother pipes up, almost hopeful.

—I found it.

—*Found? On the street?*

His mother's sobs, which had nearly subsided, renew with gusto: Not one of those corner delis!

—In my apartment building. I guess it fell out of someone's groceries.

—How do you know that for sure?

—Dad—

—How do you know it wasn't planted?

—By who? Why?

—How the hell should I know why? *To drive me crazy*—

His mother shrieks. Wendell's father's distress has
driven him halfway to his feet, where he freezes, takes stock
of his altitude; slowly, he sits back down. Then leaps
up: *What in the hell is the matter with you? What are you
thinking?*

—Darling have some milk, here. His mother pours with
one trembling hand, with the other tugs his father back to
his seat. Is your eye healing? she asks.

—For God's sake, you try to raise a kid, and just when
you think he's found himself, he's hitting his stride—

—Well, would you have preferred an orange, something
with a more obvious navel?

—Wendell, have some Yoo-Hoo, here.

—You're the sourest fruit in the Grand Union.

—Don't talk to it in front of us!

—Look, Wendell, I don't mean to insult you—

—Dad. If the apple of knowledge had been a lemon,
everything—

—Eve never would have been tempted, we'd still be
in Eden.

—You'd rather be here?

—You know what I mean.

—You're making too much of this.

—A person can't help what they feel, pleads his mother.

—Exactly!

—So we're just being honest.

—I can't understand what's so terrible about loving someone of your own species.

—Kingdom, dear.

—I'm not arguing, says Wendell. I'm sure it's blissfully convenient.

—It has proven a fairly reliable recipe.

—I don't disagree.

—And if everybody did what you do?

—They won't. Dad (he tries their old joke), can I have the keys to the piano? His father's line: *Go easy, it needs a tune-up.* Not tonight.

They sit still at the table. Then his mother, very slowly, very softly begins to weep, is quickly overcome, stumbles from her chair and out of the room. Weak, pained creaks on the stairs. Silence. A door slams.

His father says he's tired, he'd rather not drive. Can you please catch a bus. No suggestion that he stay the night, though it's unusually late. Wendell waits with the lemon on the corner half an hour for a bus, then they take the long single cushion in the rear. The vehicle is almost empty of people. Wendell places the lemon on one end of the seat, and slides to the other to look at it, the lights from outside falling over it in all colors, holiday lights still up in store windows. When the bus stops short, the lemon lurches off their seat, hits with a metallic sound the back of the one in front of them, falls and lands with a thump and rolls noisily the length of the bus, clear up to the driver's feet. Wendell follows, apologizes to the driver, who ignores him. Wendell sits near the front for the rest of the ride, the lemon in both hands. He can sense homeland agony mounting in his wake, a billowing guilt from behind. It overtakes him: when he gets home there is a message from his parents on the machine. *I hope you're having a wonderful time, please call us when it's over*—but the sarcasm doesn't hold, his mother's voice chokes and the phone slams to the floor and Wendell can hear it skidding across the tiles, smack against the wall. His father retrieves it. I wish you'd just kept this to yourself, Wendell. The problem is, you're a human being, but regardless, you're also a son. (*No he's not!*) For what it's worth, I'm trying to convince your mother that it must be love. Anything else would be absurd.

Not like Indy soma
or cocoa in Peru,
not animism;
not weed-worshipping primitivism;
we are no pueblo coma
or prance of credulous apes;
ours is a suprematism
of compatible shapes,
a civilized to-do.

Well, we don't have many in our group today, but that's all
right, it will permit me to tailor the tour for those present.
Tell me, do we have any *painted* lemons with us? Ah. Most
charming. You are a new twist on an old breed—practically
a mutant! But inevitable. We'll be looking at your family
tree today. Step this way, or roll, whatever moves you. And
please—I know sometimes a painting can look pretty
lifelike—try to refrain from touching!

The lemon has most often been portrayed intact, and can be found whole in the tombs of pharaohs and on the slopes of Roman vases, for starters. But a subtler understanding, one perhaps better revealing of the lemon's changing role in both art and life, might begin with the painted partly peeled lemon. Long a favorite motif of Western artists, its popularity peaked in the Little Dutch days of the seventeenth century, an age fascinated with the transience of life, the futility of vanity in the face of death concerns gave natural birth to the modern still-life. In the era in which these were painted—this masterpiece is by W. C. Heda— a lemon pictured a cappella might have won its maker death at the stake. As a way of diluting their idolatry, these artists were usually quite careful to provide a human context for their lemons—at the very least, they have given us visual evidence of a hand that touched and then passed on. So, on a theological plane, the partly peeled lemon is similar to the cinematic convention of cigarette butts in an ashtray to suggest the passing of time.

This work in front of us is entitled "Banquet Pieces with Mince Pie"—we can sense in every stroke the whispered haste of the party that was just here. Joyous, kinetic, now elsewhere. That lemon there on the far left of the table, three fourths peeled, you can see that while its zest curlicues off the table's edge like a strand of DNA itself, it is still attached to the fruit. The impression is of an assumption not quite complete; of an umbilical reluctance to evolve. And consider "Still Life of Parrots," this is by Heda's contemporary Jan de

Heem, in which the spiral of peel, instead of hanging freely in open space, loops back up to the table for a sense of cyclical harmony that is absent in the Heda, a resolution, a return to the source. Some of you may recognize this pose from a latterday work by Manet, if you've seen the lemon on the table of his "Luncheon Party." I myself think of both these lemons every time I see a Slinky, the popular, secularized ritualization of this pose.

It's interesting to note that Gaugin painted his own "Still Life of Parrots," in which he replaces the lemon with a small statue of Buddha. We all know where he was coming from. But in general lemons rivaled brown breasts and pomegranates for his orb of favor, and there is mention in his correspondence of a violent quarrel with Van Gogh over who could paint one with more faithfulness, though Vincent himself makes no reference to the debate in his known letters to Theo.

As the Enlightenment kicked in, so did the lemon's right to full and exclusive illumination. Bartolommeo Bimbi, court botanical painter of Cosimo III, Grand Duke of Tuscany, three centuries ago fit thirty lemons and related citrus into a grand group portrait whose fruit repose like gods, flanked with garden statues in a den of dark green foliage—quite a promotion from table corners—and Bimbi kept not only his head, but his job. Chardin raised lemons high in glorious pyramids; Bonnard coddled them in baskets; Cezanne, though he grated all fruit into facets, somehow kept their form intact. One of the nineteenth century's greatest lemon portraits was oddly enough done by Renoir, who, though he claimed he painted with his penis, in general preferred bleary saccharin to the tart and true; but he surpassed himself in his 1881 "Fruits from the Midi," whose central lemon is a feral and almost expressionist torrent of pigment. Braque—before he and Pablo smashed the world to shards and splinters, then in the thick of the wreckage, again through the course of repair—treated lemons always with reverence, posing them often with his beloved guitars. Matisse, high priest of pure color, was of course a longtime lover—lemons are everywhere in his oeuvre.

Where are you now, in art? Not easily found. Or am I just stodgimental for the knowns? And blind to my own times, such is sanity's scheme. But your career as a model seemed at least threatened the day Warhol chose a soup can, which didn't wobble when the subway tore by. Though each of those cans has a big yellow dot smack in the center, like a lemon foreshortened.

—He's not, is he?
—No he's not, but she is.
—Well at least she is.
—But he's not.
A large room of etchings that appear to be by Rembrandt—some are, some aren't. A curatorial exploration of McCoy & Mimic, many of the "fakes" having been made

for honest reasons by the master's peers and pupils. Wendell and the lemon are in the line of trudging gazers, just behind a conversation taking place in the etchings' protective glass. In between works, facing the white wall, the speakers pause. Then find each other again in the next reflection.

—Everything else seems perfect.

—What about the children?

—Please.

—The modern world.

—I don't like all those little marks.

—Cross-hatching.

—Fussy, nervous.

—You don't think subtle?

—Inferior medium. The tragedy is, they're perfectly happy.

Wendell has gradually come to notice that the lemon is functioning as a dowser. When he stands in front of a print and feels an increased pressure against his palm, he checks the information card and finds, almost invariably, that the work has been deemed authentic; if the lemon doesn't budge, the etching is by someone else.

—It's a generational phenomenon. Happiness has lost all touch with quality.

—Do you think it's genuine happiness?

—Oh, it definitely is (on to the next etching), that's the tragedy of it.

—Is that a dog?

They squint, crane closer. Scoop backward.

—It looks like a cow.

—That's what I thought, but in a haystack?

—A cow's more likely than a dog.

—A crow *is* more likely.

—But it won't fit like that.

—A dog or a cat or a bird. Happiness is no longer a moral issue. These people go right ahead without any regard for those around them. What does it say?

—I can't see the print.

—Oh they're happy all right, but not why they think they are— "Divided." Well I'm not divided, that's no Rembrandt, Rembrandt knew the difference between dogs and cows.

—Don't be so sure— Oh!

—What?

—It isn't a haystack!

—Of course it is.

—No, it's a—I think it's a library.

Wendell steps up behind and between them. I can assure you, he says, that what you behold is a bona-fide Rembrandt.

—Do you work here?

Sanctus Citrus! Unemployment the only natural state. On to Goya, whose grotesquities offer some perspective on Wendell's own drooping puss. Then in the cafeteria they sit near the condiment counter near a stately bowl of lemon wedges. Ah—! Wearing the same shirt I was on the day I found you. Hermes be nigh.

Abstraction in the Twentieth Century. Exorbitant Special Admission Fee but you are free, iota. Huh? Everything after Kandinsky a curlicue? Sour on the century, are you? Let's into this side gallery, shall we, and behold the Permanent.

What's this here, a still-life of lemons by Braque coming down from Cubism, yes here's eternal, yes. Protagonist's left uppercut thrust reminiscent of yours in the soap holder, yes. Here's balance, here's friction. One stick will never get you fire, unless you're struck by lightning, but then you might not be around to make use of it. I was here last with Marge, for a similar parade of ambivalent hype, and our earthbound chat after solitary ascents: *Who was it, the guy who made the cockroach clock? Roach eats its own excrement in a circle, moves the hands—*

— *A Russian, I think.*

—*That's what this is.*

—*We have to get new traps.*

—*We did.*

—*We didn't.*

—*They should at least have a picture of that here. Art for roaches.*

—*We could stop on the way home.*

—*We could stop at that place for sandwiches.*

No I won't discuss this, anything I say is false because I know the truth too well. Talk about traps. Facts' fools! Drowning in our day-to-day, hard data the only handy floatable. Shameful. We're dealing with the species that signs, here! We've digitized the world, now let's have the crux!

Some points are piñatas.

Yourself? No dimensions or three?

You know there are transitional dimensions, c/o Mandelbrot: 1.2, 3.5, etc.

I'd peg you at a four-two.

Or—?

All my school geometry moot. Fortunately my mind was elsewhere—on you, though we didn't yet know it. O sweet sour. So used to imagining nothingness as black space, you make me see the reverse might be true, that before anything else there was solid light. (No *room* for time? What ruptures light? Brick wall.) Last night I had a dream of us both dangling from the same tree—you, me, and a cell phone. Speaking the lost tongue of flowers. Unanswerable questions, godlike indifference. My how you shine, lucky tango! You have merged with the world, taken its will within you, some would say fallen but we know plucked. All is aphrodesia. Bring on the Apocalypse! You are my found object.

Here is a way to capture and kill roaches. They like beer.
Pour some in a bowl. Set it down in their agora. Prop broom
straws against the edge, balanced so that if a thirsty roach
should climb one, the weight of its zeal will topple the
straw and it into the beer, where it will drown.
But you need a broom. And you need to give a damn.
Priorities change.
Thw world is a blizzard of catalysts.

In the park by the river in the middle of the night by the
after-hours light of a boathouse, he Scotch tapes lemon to a
see-saw and they ride for hours, then fall to the grass and lay
in its rustling till daybreak. A taxi to the outskirts—
Seatbelt? Ha! Safety is danger serene and supreme, thrust
you out the window, feel that wind?—and a corner table for
the breakfast set of a jazz band that's been lubing all night.
Nice. If you're gonna cover standards, do it with a twist.
Lemon you are the best companion, we can do tabletop keys

along with these guys without distracting them, you're such a quiet thumper. Look, house chess-set. That candle shows you nicely.

Wendell opens, King's pawn out two. That song has a name—do we? Lemon from queenside, several pieces at once, two off the catty corner, a brilliant if unorthodox Sicilian variation. Player leaves the table. Wendell scoops it up from the floor, his hair singeing on somebody's cigarette, the room is hot and crowded, band is cooking, lemon back on the table on the other side of the board, navel eyes him— what botanists call "the remains of style." Look at this board! Puck, what have ye wrought? Takes him minutes to formulate a response, time spent reasoning back to instinct. Conservative, but lemon's next roll forces him to reconsider yet again. *I've got a crush on you, sour Pi.* He scrambles for a familiar position. Resigns after lemon's fourth move.

"There is no remorse like the remorse of chess. It annihilates a man." False conclusion of H. G. Wells. No war of worlds here. A postmate regret full of joy and wonder; I celebrate your win as my own.

Nope, won't sing along with this one. Shouldn't punish the song for the foibles of the singer, but for me it just reeks. Sinatra detested "Strangers in the Night," that classic record was pure commerce. All those "doo-be-doo-be-doos"— nothing behind 'em. Marge called this fact a true American koan. She sure could sing the tune great, though. She had this astounding ability. We used to take walks in the park along the river, and in the spring there was a mockingbird, always in the same bush, he'd be going on, this incredibly varied repertoire of calls, he'd be singing, we'd stop and listen and Marge would whistle back, and she did him to a T, it was like two birds jamming, it was beautiful.

What have we here? Every time I see you, even if I've just blinked, it's like all the other times I've seen you all on top of each other with a cherry. It wasn't at first sight that I knew, but in retrospect I see it happened then. At my feet you appeared, silent matter—I reached for you. To my squeeze you yielded fear, grief, uncertainty, the steady tripod of my hope. Bartender may I take a slice? Just the slice —thank you. Here, I'll squeeze— Have you ever seen lemon juice? From without? Of course you have. But watch this: If we dip this twizzler in it—

On a damp square napkin he draws a circle with lemon juice, and inside it, using lemon's length as his unit measure, Leonardo's sprawled-man study of human proportions. Twenty tall, I am. MUS OGRE SURTIC.

At home with water-soluble fingerpaint they impersonate a lime, apple, basketball, earth, sun, Saturn, Jupiter; they do the geodesic dome and a Fabergé egg. A few soda straws and they solve the problem of tripedal locomotion. Discovery: you sit neatly in the cup of my eye-patch, I can swing you in circles to make a yellow hoop in the air.

Does he dream or does it happen that Fuller calls him late at night, he has become smitten with a tangerine. They meet at a bar and the man is in tears, fawning over the fruit which he carries in a bowling-ball case. Wendell is coolly unforgiving as Fuller drunkenly weeps, frantic for his own future, begging mercy for his past treatment of Wendell. *I had already reached Damascus.* Wendell assures him it is probably only a vitamin deficiency and Fuller offers him his job back. *Just as you're connecting the last dots you realize you've been drawing on the wrong side of the page.* Instead of one working eye, Wendell has three, seeing Fuller simultaneously from above and behind and frontally, Wendell is himself an insect, beer-bottle size; he flies with lemon to the center of the floor where they boogie in midair to the jukebox.

They reenact his finding it, late at night at the same hour, at different hours, in the morning with people scraping past them, dogs tripping the lemon into rolling. You arrived; I arrived; you were there when I entered, you were motionless, your future could be anything. The door swung open, my foot appeared, my shin, my knee, I entered, there I was, there you were. Here you are. There I was. My big yellow marble. My scrofula, my nebula, my nebulous chum. I'm a shark. Here comes my gape, I got you. You're a shark too. You were thorny. You prickled me. You were very soft, I sensed you around me, you were everywhere.

Go, fingertips. With all my skin, with all my blood, with all my brains, with all my brawn. This is the world we live on, these its mountains, valleys, pools. We to play. Rock the Baby, Walk the Dog, Golden Goose, Atlas, Human Asymptote, Freezing Eskimo versus the Sealed Igloo, Foucault's Pendulum, Rock Star Groin, Particle Accelerator,

Benign Tumor, Zeno Crosses the Room, Name That Sex, Alas Poor Yorick, Venus in Furs, Crotch Hockey, Eye of the Hurricane, How Long Is the Coast of Britain, Neil Armstrong's Views from Space, Flesh Hanging from Soul Clinging to Air Inhaled of Earth Spun from Stars That Rush from Deep Wisdom Like Fruit from the Tree, Babes from the Womb.

Wendell loses, finds, and finally opens the envelope Michelle gave him on his last day at work, scrunched, his name laundered to near illegible. Inside is soberly typed info on a beach house owned by friends who don't use it during winter. They love to have people stay there to keep an eye on it, as sometimes there are damaging storms. Storms, citrus! Nothing's ever sounded better. He dials the number, hoping he hasn't waited too long, finds that Michelle's friends are enthusiastic to hear from him, he can have the place through early March, a few weeks. Wendell packs that night and leaves the next day. The house is right on the water, and the beach in the off-season is deliciously clean and deserted.

IV

Such light here! Gentlest hints of dawn nudge us from sleep, the glass walls bringing sea and sky right into the room. From our pillows we watch the stars gray over, then the hush of blue into gold and the pinkening of the bellies of clouds. The sun itself, red like a grapefruit, directly watchable for a full hour while rising. Bundle of my true juice. I dreamed that a juggler got hold of you and tossed you with bayonets.

Once in grade school I stuck copper and zinc into one of your kind, whose innards turned electrolyte and lit up a small lightbulb for half an hour. On you I can feast without depleting. It's my energy that's spent, good for the chi. Takes me a joule to lift you one yard; American, I daily exert myself six thousand percent more than I would if I lived in my corresponding caste in India, land of your forefruit.

What's that? Fruit on the branch wants to be picked? That's what it lives for? Life on the tree is a vigil? There's a palpable yearning to be eaten, a constant leaning outward from the branch?

But it wasn't always this way. The open hand of an arm extended. The stirrings of gravity. A grasping and dismemberment, a branch snapping back, bobbing. A loss, a gain. Then came a day when a sick fruit was plucked; the eater died; relations since have been delicate.

You look positively clitoral this morning, smudge, you make me wonder again—this skin: female hue of some tropical hotbed of evolution? Or your salient singularity: phallic? Breast? But acid/lactate dissonance dwarfs your shape, and as for feel— If I am allergic to Freud, does that prove him right?

No. Truth sheds trivia. Ain't it so, Googolus?

Scenario for a Seduction: *S'ex Nihilo.*

If the Universe at its smallest level is space and spheres. So then the Universe self-assembled through the interplay of spheres. So then what was that like. Spheres moving among spheres, touching, one point of touching any one other at a time, touching others, a ballet of globes.

Feel like dangling in the doorway? Chance moves you more sagely than I, I know. Can nirvana be approached other than by asymptote?

I'll fill you with music now. Steady . . . Someday there will be the technology to bathe the whole earth in the same song, an earphone on each polar cap.

= = =

Next month, the sun and six planets will line up like billiard balls in a configuration that could shift the poles, trigger earthquakes, crash the stock market, and usher in the Age of Aquarius if anyone survives. Mercury, Venus, Mars, all of us will be the culprits, though we won't be able to tell from here, the sun will be too bright. Not to fear, people! I hold you up like this, we block the rays.

Down to the beach to where the tide is breaking, firm but not violent, at regular intervals. The sand is packed hard and clean, an occasional shell and claw spotting the surface. A living museum of miracles. No one else in sight. A crime and a blessing. At the water's edge he lightly pitches the lemon a few feet out into the ocean. The next small wave slaps it back to his feet in a foamy churl. He picks it up, it is cold, he brushes some sand from its barrel and repeats the toss, this time throwing it a bit farther out, so that it requires the push of several gentle waves to wash it back to him; the tide is at an angle, he has to jog a few yards to catch up.

The next day he buys a disposable camera and photographs the lemon in the sea. He throws it farther each time, and stops when he becomes afraid it's going too far to return; but thinks he's got the shot he wanted, from a crouching position: lemon silhouetted on the horizon, a great sloped ship.

They move to dry sand, where he buries it up to its nipple. With shells and pebbles he creates a wreath on the sand out to a radius of several feet, then holds the camera over his head to catch the arrangement in whole.

The sky bruises purple, thunder comes, and hard rain. Quick, we'll miss our plane! Why wasn't it delayed, in such vexatious weather? Have to get this sand off you or they won't let us board—Ah!—missed it. There she goes, our flight; we are here. That's fine. We'll sit and watch the others take off, their lights' reflections descending in the bay like runaway souls. Hope there's water where those planes are headed, hope of reunion.

Run, lemon! Along the rim of lapping surf!

Spring is near some days, though on most Wendell can still see his breath. They walk far along the shore. How many times each day do tourists in Rome say or think "When in Rome"? Wanna know everything, do ya?

One mild afternoon, after heading north for several miles along the water, a boardwalk begins, leads soon into a stretch of shops, game booths, the ruins of a small amusement park. Boarded up cartoon structures, DANGER signs. Some maybe just closed or the season? One arcade with few display lights blinking; its door unlocked: HANSEL'S WORLD OF LUCK. They enter.

Inside there is no sign of life apart from a steady mesh of beeping and humming from hundreds of electronic game stations, and countless Wendells and lemons reflected in the mirrored walls that cause the room to seem even vaster than it is—endless. Making no sound of their own on the thinly carpeted floor, they walk the aisles under low mirrored ceilings, looking at the machines, their flashing beckonings and promises.

A door squeaks behind a display counter; there is a glitch in the mirrored infinity; a stooped man in a checkered golf cap appears carrying a newspaper. He settles on a stool and reads, one more silent figure among the rows of stuffed prize animals ceiling-high on the wall behind him, palm-size to giant. The man gives no sign of being aware of Wendell and the lemon.

Wendell fishes a quarter from his pocket and sits at a 25-cent slot machine about ten yards away from the man. He places lemon on top of the machine, blows on his quarter for luck. But it won't fit in the slot.

—Tokens only, the man says. He does not look up from his paper. His hand rises and points toward a machine, tokens for money.

Wendell changes a dollar, sits back down, plays. He loses three tokens, then on his fourth he wins, he wins big. But no noise, no gleaming flood, no hoopla. So it was for most at Klondike. He looks at the man: Excuse me.

The man looks up. His eyes are very bright, and beam right in on Wendell's machine. He recognizes Wendell's tone, knows what he wants.

—Three in a row.

—You want cherries to win, the man says, looking back down into his paper. Three lemons is triple-*lose*. And then he sharply looks up again, his gaze hawking in on the lemon on top of Wendell's machine. He watches it for a very brief moment, something seeming to click in his brain. Then he looks back down into the newspaper.

Nocturnal tentacles out of the past. Crossing a river on a bridge into the city. Tollbooths manned by construction workers in heavy yellow rain slickers that hood them faceless. He drops change into ceramic vats caked in soot and rain, and swims naked through the gate into an indoor pool of mud and spinach. He is told to swim faster so as not to wake the vicious dogs that sleep just under the surface. Dog breath bubbles the mud, warming the pool. Other swimmers churn along beside him, it is rush hour, all lanes converge at the far end of the pool where there is a small opening in a muddied stucco wall, through which they swim one by one to find themselves standing dry, wearing comfortable white cotton long underwear, in a cavernous neon-lit room. Huge rusted support beams enforest the space, it must be basement level, a parking lot. Clusters of people form to chat, familiar faces, postures, phrases. They are waiting. Wendell settles on a soft warm couch, nestles himself among several others, all of them white-clad, maggotlike. A television faces them, whooshing after-hours static, and, still dreaming, Wendell awakens to the face of his father, who smiles at Wendell, then past him.

Wendell turns and sees rising from the couch a woman of his own age, he has seen her only once before on line on the sidewalk outside of a restaurant years ago, he has never seen her again, he remembers noticing her in this same way—his father's affectionate glance directed behind him, a father's good wish for his son. And now this same majesterial sprite, whose face he has until now forgotten, rises from the couch (she has been sleeping there) and slowly stands, her knees unbending, her legs bare and straightening. She stands in two pieces of underwear, unfolding herself from sleep, her navel a drowsy eye, her body a woman's body, her face flushed with sleep, hair dusking her shoulders. She stretches, her fingertips twittering toward the ceiling. Red and white shoot and splash across her just-risen flesh, tendons flexing. All white and blood red, she is, her bottom dappled by the tatters of the couch. Rising, standing, straightening, stretching, turning in his general direction, saying goodnight. She walks away. After a moment he says to his father, or to himself or to the air, that he will follow, and he rises and heads after her, through spacious stairwells full of echoes, he follows her up, up, listening to her bare feet snapping on the cold stone steps, her buttocks and legs flexing, abdomen creasing and flattening, he knows the beads of sweat on her forehead following the furrows of her concentration, eyes fixed on feet, her hair breezing across her cheeks and catching in the sheen of sweat and bunching on her shoulders, nostrils flaring for oxygen, the thrum of blood in her veins.

He follows her through a door. In a small low-ceilinged room she greets a man rising from the bed at the far end of the room. They embrace, and she pulls out of it turning toward Wendell to make introductions—?

Bright morning and he is awake in the beach house, lemon beside him in sunlight. He turns to it, his shifting weight bearing down on the pillow it is on. Hills and valleys change places and lemon rises from its niche. Moving forward to meet it, his mussed hair causes gossamer shadows to pass like clouds over yellow plains.

Wendell feels buoyed, afloat on a malted sea, effortlessly healthful, warmth cascading from the top of his head down along his left jaw to his chin. One day, walking the beach with lemon swinging in the eye-patch, he realizes his blinks are providing momentary darkness, equal darkness in both eyes. At home in the mirror his smile is almost symmetrical and his left eye three quarters its old aperture. Can health be such a quick sprint away, a few weeks' peace? Hang the patch on the bathroom doorknob. Save it for Carnaval. Sits in the sun with lemon over his right eye to allow the left's color to catch up.

Side by side on the couch. A diamond of sunlight on the wall, the motion of its upward climb discernible during these quick last minutes of sunset; the trapezoid narrows and elongates as hot tea is sipped on the couch. On the radio a Mozart French horn concerto in D. More than just the twinkling sharps, there is something in its wavelengths that suggest a familiar spectrum. The horn is warm, not as yellow as trumpet. Redder, musky, more like the tea.

Stars appear in bright brambles on night's lawn; here and there one ripens and falls into the ocean. You were such a star. A fireball that fought to reach my planet. And I a stagnant sea, my caked stasis punctured. A sizzle, a splash, a cooling and plunge to depths. Your wake a forged hollow scope. I look through. Below me you rest serene, unmoved by currents.

No clocks, no phone, only time blossoming from its center, stretching freely toward all horizons. Time not pushed or tugged by its liver. The weight of the sun as it passes underneath. The hairs on your arms standing and leaning toward the moon as it rises. We look and the air sucks our gaze and keeps sucking, the black mouth of space wolfs us. Everywhere we look, an oscillating field. We speak and remember and speak. Life is a single day on one planet. We are a reed.

On the main street that spines the peninsula, outside the town's only bar. It's a brisk spring night with a salty breeze from off the sea, and they are still for a moment, taking it all in. With two eyes the world seems huge. Lemon in his hands inside the pocket that runs across the front of his sweatshirt. The whoosh of the surf a block away overlaps and blends with the engine of an approaching car that passes packed with teenagers yelling, and recedes down the long wide road.

Inside the bar the band concludes a set to indifferent applause. A crooner takes over on the jukebox. They walk around the corner of the white-slatted building, see on it their shadow large by the moon coming up over the ocean, a thin arch with its back to the water. Turning in the other direction, they can look down the cross-street to the opposite shore, bayside, where low in the sky a brilliant light hovers.

—That's Venus, Sputnik.

They walk toward the splendid planet, across the main street and west down to the bay, where they sit on a bench on the plank sidewalk between the road and the sand. They watch the planet set into the mists and lights of many small towns. Water laps lightly, quick odd rhythms.

Standing, turning again toward the darker oceanside, they head slowly back toward the bar, the late-night lulls of the jukebox faintly audible. As they cut through a small parking lot across the street from the bar, bright lights pierce them from behind and a car swings into the lot. On the bar's white side their shadow is quick and monstrous from the headlights. The bulge of lemon at his stomach.

A male voice, gruff, official: Who's that?

Wendell turns, sees only fierce light; the car is less than ten feet away. The voice has come from the driver's side. Wendell holds up an arm to shield his eyes, moves sideways out of the light.

—Hey! fires the voice. You don't leave.

Wendell pauses just outside of the headlights' glare, near the rear of a parked police car. Then he sees that the parking lot is filled with police cars; that the driver is addressing him from one; that a pistol has been drawn.

—Oh please, you don't need to do that.

—What are you doing here?

—I came out for some air. We were in the bar—right over there. He turns to gesture.

—Stay where you are, please.

Wendell has the impression of the gun nodding at him. The officer turns his car into a space, parks, kills the lights, gets out. With the headlights off, the night looks normal again in streetlamp light, stars visible. He can see the man now as he approaches: large, generously mustached, holstering his gun—this seems to Wendell somehow as aggressive an action as cocking it would have been—then looping his thumbs through his belt: Who you with?

—Just myself. Just getting some air, a little walk.

—You said "we" were in the bar, who's we?

—Just a figure of speech.

—Huh. You the president?

—It was crowded in the bar.

—Take your hands out of your shirt there, please.

Slowly Wendell withdraws his hands from the front pocket of his sweatshirt, leaving lemon inside. He raises his palms toward the officer; but the man's attention has remained on the bulging fabric. He moves slowly to within a few feet of Wendell, stands squarely before him. In what seems like the single most deranged act Wendell has ever known, the officer raises one gloved hand, removes the glove finger by finger with the other, flexes them once, reaches toward Wendell's sweatshirt pocket, and through the thin cotton gingerly folds his hand around the bulge.

—What is this?

—A lemon.

—Remove it from your shirt, please—slow.

223

Cop backs away a few steps, hand on holster. Wendell takes the lemon from his shirt, holds it out on his palm. The officer bends a little at the knees to better examine the fruit at close range. He scrutinizes all sides of the lemon without touching it. His mustache an anemone in the rising wind.

—I was in the bar and it got smoky. I came out for some air. Didn't realize this was a police parking lot. I would've walked the other way.

The officer unbends, says, If you knew this was a police station you would have deliberately avoided it?

—I just don't mean to disrespect.

—You always carry a lemon around?

—Yes sir.

—You do.

—This one I do.

—What's wrong with it.

—It's painted.

—Come with me, please. He gestures for Wendell to precede him into the back door of the tiny stationhouse.

—But I've done nothing.

Wendell and the policeman walk through a narrow hall, full of red shadows, into a well-lit office near the front of the station where another cop sits with his jacket off and legs up on the desk, hands linked behind his neck, watching dirt bike races on a high-mounted television.

Wendell's escort falls into a ragged black vinyl rollchair and unbuttons the top of his trousers. You know this person, George?

George, who looks to Wendell much too young to have a subtle grasp of law, looks him down and up.

Leaning against the doorframe, Wendell says to Mustache, No, he doesn't know me, and to George: I was across the street at the bar and I came out for some air. I was walking through the parking lot of your station. I touched no vehicle.

—Haven't had the pleasure.

Mustache swivels in his chair to face Wendell. Where you from?

—I'm just down here, I came down for a few weeks, friend's house. This is my last night in town.

—Show my partner what you got in your pocket. Mustache turns to George. He was out in the lot. Thought he was messin' with one of your trucks.

—It's only a lemon. Wendell holds it up for George to see.

—He had that in his pocket.

—It's no grenade, Wendell ventures, demonstrates his new symmetrical smile, though with a whisper of tug on the left. But he can relax; he hasn't done anything wrong. Two cops trying to do their job.

George lifts his feet off the desk, settles them on the concrete floor, leans toward Wendell. Lemme see.

—Just a lemon.

—Please.

—I'm telling you.

George holds out his hand. Wendell places the lemon on the palm. George brings it near to his eyes, peruses closely, squinches. Says, What's wrong with it?

—I painted it.

—What for?

—To keep it fresh, sort of.

—Larry, you see this? He places it on the corner of his desk.

—Yeah, I know. Larry wheels himself over and looks at the lemon. George rummages through papers on his desktop and finds a pencil, with which he taps the lemon first with the writing end, then the eraser. He is not satisfied. He picks up the lemon, bounces it lightly on the desk blotter from about half an inch up.

—Please don't.

The officers look at him, then at each other.

George says, Interesting.

Larry picks up the lemon. Gimme that light. George swings his overhead lamp closer—stark shadows careen through the room—and shines it on the lemon. Larry taps the lemon with the side of the pencil, holds it up to his ear, gingerly jiggles it.

—That really isn't necessary, Wendell says. It's a lemon.

—You wanna tell us what this is?

—I'm telling you, it's stuffed with some newspaper to hold its shape, then glued together and painted over. That's Scotch tape under the surface for texture, and some salt.

—Lemme see that. George takes the lemon from Larry and shakes it vigorously next to his ear. Could be a Molotov-type thing.

—Are you serious?

—Just mind what's not your business.

Larry: Then we probably shouldn't shake it, huh? And he takes the lemon back from George, puts it down on the desk.

—It's a lemon. I found it one day and kept it and it got a little brown so I painted it, and now I just carry it around.

—For luck?

—Something like that.

—I've seen weirder, says George, and Larry: I doubt it.

—Maybe it's not so weird.

—It's too light to be Dangerous dangerous.

—There are different kinds of danger.

—Look, the only danger is to me.

—That's what I'm saying.

—So can I have it back?

George is fishing in a drawer for something. He finds it: a small rock hammer.

—That's good, says Larry.

—Aren't you guys able to tell when a person is being straight with you? Isn't that part of what you do?

—Watch television, do ya?

—If it's what you say it is we'll buy you a whole new sack of brand new good-luck charms.

Larry positions the lemon on the edge of the desk, and holds it while George taps it a few times with the rock hammer.

Wendell moves from his spot in the door and starts toward the lemon, but Larry is fast in his rollchair, blocks him. Grabs a billystick off a wall hook. You got it? he says to George.

—Yeah.

Larry, still seated, places the end of the billystick on Wendell's chest just under the hollow of his neck; then slowly stands, keeping the stick-end focussed.

—I'm telling you guys. That lemon means a lot to me, I know it sounds weird but you can't imagine, it's like a family heirloom.

—You told us you found it.

—You want me to pay a fine? Wendell's body feels cold. Hot. I'll pay you whatever you want. I'm leaving tomorrow.

—You listening to this guy? Poppin' the seeds, or whaddya think?

—Actually, Wendell says, growing giddy, "pips" is the word for lemon seeds, and it's an interesting thing, the word is short for pippin, which actually refers to a kind of an apple, a cooking apple, and also has a second meaning, an admired person or thing.

—Dare I say good grief.

—Look, if I had anything in there, what would I be doing around a police parking lot?

—Man, just let us do our job here.

—You told us you didn't know it was a police parking lot.

—That lemon means a lot to me, officers. I swear.

—That is evident.

—So—

—You are a stranger discovered snooping around a police parking lot in the middle of the night in what is not tourist season, then we find what appears to be a lemon but

228

is in fact some type of encasement wherein it is painted to resemble a lemon, then you get the shakes when we question you about it, then you beg us—beg, mind you—that we shouldn't search any farther?

—But didn't you ever have some kind of something, some unreasonable attachment to something?

—Ha! I'll say! George seems to find this hysterically funny. During his coughing fit, Wendell lunges again for the lemon, but Larry shoves him back with the stick. Wendell stumbles backward, catches the chair with the heel of his hand, finds purchase.

—You'd rather be handcuffed to the chair? Go ahead, he directs George.

—Please, no, please.

George leans over the lemon. He taps it with the hammer, twice, firmly.

—Careful.

—I can give you the phone numbers of people who know me, they'll tell you I'm an odd person with an attachment to this lemon. I'm allowed one phone call, aren't I? But you make the call. That's fine with me.

Their attention is no longer on him.

Wendell's vision is swimmingly useless but still he turns away when he hears the hammer smack the painted casement, a pause, then again, then then again, cracking it with the sound of candy shell fracturing on teeth. Bits of dry paint fall dully onto the desk blotter and a blink later sharp on the floor, but he can hear that the lemon has not yielded its shape. The hammer hits again, a webbier sound, more flakes fly, one of them hitting the back of his neck. The lemon is harder than he'd have expected, it resists, this gives him a fleeting and futile satisfaction. He hears a vexed grunt, then a pair of thwacks of the lemon skull struck by hand against the edge of the desk, a pause, then fresher surface hitting wood, and again, again, the lemon rotated to intact shell with each strike—but not opening to their anger, maybe it's the tape layer. Foggily he hears them confer, their frustration growing, they discuss sawing the lemon open or even shooting it or at least he thinks this is what he hears, has heard, for his ears have seized on the roar of motorbikes on television, and everything else in the room seems muffled. Then a powerful hand gripping his shoulder and pulling him up and out of the room into green corridor neon with a gaping blackness afloat and footsteps echoing through a door and out again into the parking lot, cold wind snaps his cheeks. Whose face does he see? Blank and static and sure, but not blank the tires on the wheels of the car that is moving, that rubber is deep-treaded, and here are the throes of his very own amazement at the reeling back-ing-up of these tires, back and forth rubber in flashlight glare scrambling day and night, the fury of suspicion confounded by innocence, the shattering of shells and gurgling organs, a grand piano tumbles down a flight of stairs, his own hands stuffed in fire gripped by forbidding bulk behind him, inability to move forward, he is only eyes and colossal will toward No, then drooping long-necked perplexity, a couple of dollar bills lazy, wafting, a long time fluttering, to the pavement.

The beach is white in all directions as far as he can see, thick white cloud through everything, the sun nowhere and everywhere. He sits up on the bench. His eyes can't make out the ocean, but the surf is loud, wild; he stands, achy, walks toward the sound, down a slope of sand to where the water seems to spill from the sky, a heavier condensation of the fog. All is thinness and thickness of white, horizonless foam churning in sea and sky, no horizon. Seagulls not knowing where to dive circle in air above gnawing water. Feathers all whites and grays as if selected by nature for chalky days like this, when the fight for food is fiercest. A squawk above—then the mangled blue-pink carcass of a crab falls at his feet. A gull emerges into view coasting a tight circle, cawing. Wendell walks backward, giving the gull room, but it recedes spiraling into the fog before he can see what it does. He turns and walks on, looking out toward the invisible sea. Somewhere out there is the Titanic, resting in peace until the next pillage, unless one is happening now. Sixteen thousand lemons sunk with her. Fish have tastebuds on their heads and all over their bodies. A car pulls up at the end of one of the roads that lead to the ocean, parallel headlight beams slicing the fog. A door opens and a little girl in a blue raincoat and shiny red rain hat climbs out and runs across the boardwalk, down toward the water. She frightens a few gulls, not much smaller than herself, into flight. She is just a few yards in front of him, but has not seen him. She runs the opposite way down the beach, screaming happily when the foam soaks her shoes; then, like a lure cast and trailed, she turns from the ocean and runs straight back toward the car and gets in, and the car drives off with a triangle of blue peeping from the bottom crack of door. Out of the sky cuts the arc of a Ferris wheel, then the whole wheel, then other careening silhouettes of the amusement park, and the rides move through the fog in smooth small jerks, the way he moves through the next few days, in and out of sleep and hunger and memory. A bus ride. Himself in the city sitting on his suitcase on the subway platform, the remains of the lemon in a plastic bag in his lap. After midnight. A few people waiting for the trains, sleeping on benches. The sound of spraying water advances, then comes the scraping of stiff broom bristles on asphalt, then the bristles themselves, long, brown, industrial, on the top steps of the flight from the platform above. Sudsy water appears and spills and is pushed by brooms, whisked in gusts and sweeping spurts down the steps toward the platform. Soap bubbles swirling in the rushing water, the cleaning crew descending too, in boots of heavy black rubber. Vested like bees, like Halloween candy, orange over dark overalls, sloshing. More light now, a train is coming, from where he can't tell. The yellow lines along the edge of the platform run chipped and sooty black into the tunnels, uptown, downtown.

On the table a card from Marge under her returned set of apartment keys: **YOU COULD HAVE TOLD ME YOU LET MY PLANTS DIE, YOU WOULD HAVE SAVED ME A TRIP.**

The ceiling jowls toward him like a rain-laden tarp. He opens the window, flops on his back on the couch in a scream of sun, dust flying; sifts through his mail. Something from Payroll, hand-addressed. Michelle. A magazine article printed off the Internet, dated the year before his birth. Circled in blue crayon is a paragraph that describes corporate executives in a training program, each handed a lemon and told to look and look. All the lemons are then thrown into the center of the room. *"Go get your lemon," said the trainer. Each participant's citrus stood out from its fellows as clearly as a lover's face . . .* The Lemon Test, they called it. At the foot of the page is the word PRECEDENT, in crayon. Well, well. Attached, on a separate page:

There once was a lemon who couldn't
And then it was told that it shouldn't.
Then it did—with a roar!
And the world begged for more
And the lemon quite suddenly wouldn't.

Bills, bills, bills—and Sally and Bill: engaged. Brief handscrawled hellos.

On the kitchen counter are the two halves of the lemon he bought during the winter, out that night for the holiday singalong, dark and dry as paper, they sit like staring spiderwebbed skull eyes.

Nothing.

Brown and brittle and foreign, all they do is exist.

After days of unending sight-lines, of stars and stretches of beach and a house with room to dance in, expand in, the closeness of his home turf is cruel. Air is frightfully scarce here. What is visible of himself in the mirror is still limber, symmetrical; but he is apprehensive. The urge to be out beneath sky is great.

He leaves the apartment, walks. Crosses the street to avoid the rant of Gloria. Birdsong in that tree, lean sparrows. *Hey, where's your tomato? There he goes, Tomato Man.*

Countless unbroken windows vouch a drought of passion in my city.

= = =

He closes Asylum for the umpteenth consecutive night, but no quantity of souse can muffle the fact that the soloist in his ceiling has mutated into a small chamber orchestra. Wendell wants to be alone. When the exterminator knocks, Wendell lets him in, tells him to take care of the roaches once and for all.

—I do it right, you shouldn't sleep here tonight.

—I won't.

He strolls miles along the river until the night is late and he finds himself in the business district at the foot of its most regal hotel, which he enters, slipping past dozing security into the Grand Ballroom, where he sleeps in the stage wings under the tent of a draped baby grand, sneakers wrapped in shirt for pillow. Is awakened mid-morning to the brustling hum of floor waxers.

His apartment a smoky battlefield. Wendell does what he must with the charnel. A grim undertaking that fills three Cup O' Noodles cups with little and not so little corpses.

Wendell is eminently employable, skilled and seasoned, a headhunter's dream. He can afford to take his time. Enrolls with a temp agency. *Warren, would you fax these for me?* A variety of indistinguishable days.

And to the inevitable questions, what will I say? When they ask, will I answer Crushed or Dead or Finished and accept condolences, sincere, condescending, uncomprehending; will I reply with formal grace tinged with mirth to accommodate or deny my comforters? Will I attempt to explain my late mate, inert and insentient, and by these very nullities more pabulum to my days than any conceivable organismal peer?

For when he thinks of ostensible steps up on the maturational hierarchy of love, gauged by the standards of seeming feedback, interaction, interplay of senses; when he imagines time spent with a paramecium, say, or parrot or snail or a Venus flytrap, the promise of motion and perception seems bleak and muddied and miserably slow. Such creatures' brute proportions of higher qualities immediately evoke their own limits. And if at one imagined step on the road toward conscious kinetics the border lights are already flashing—

Who would trade our roots in Chance?

= = =

To the freezer. Inside, nesting in Tupperware embedded in frost, is all I have left of you. I take you out.

Thawed contents fiercely pungent in the morning, bacteria back to business, your vestiges splayed on the porcelain ledge of the bathtub where I lie in hot water now cooled to room temperature. The finish of your thaw drips down over and into shredded rind in mashes and streaks, shards of painted shell popped loose from skin, back flaps speckled with convex relief from the pressure of salt crystals, unsticky sinews of gnarled tape twists spasmodically patched with clusters of salt and street-grit, crumpled pods of newsprint guts with letters smudged by sperm to gray nonsense, five lemon pips, brown, very much pips.

With your mangled maw and ancient innards, your soggy newsprint and girdled shell for fill; the scraped-bare halves of Storebought for skin, and, for soul and sealant, new doublestick tape and paint and salt, I make new fruit from the wreckage of old. It dries seamlessly.

Lay eyes will never know the difference.

= = =

I am human, after all. There are assumptions I must make, in order to function. The truth is not the most practical field of consideration, not as long as Time's around. There is biology, there are imperatives. I can tweak both to some extent.

You. You *were*. You *have been*.
If you were already—
Never.
If you were that through which I—
I.
I *am*.
I *made* you.
No.
Chaos *becomes* you.
Do I believe that?
You were always it.
It.
Who?

And this in my hand? Facsimile. Not in hope or from any deep need have I fashioned this thing, this hodgepodge of my lately life, same sphere pulled to two pinches again and again.

Maybe tomorrow I will feel, want, know. Will I yield to the destiny of continuous matter, flow like a leaf in swift currents, free, determined, perpendicular to time, tomorrow?

Cauldron of my lost voices, bubble and steam!

Soon. For today: craft. To maintain appearances.

Today I am all practicality.